T0166646

Sentimental Exorcisms

David Derry

Coach House Books | Toronto

Published with the generous assistance of the Canada Council for the Arts and the Ontario Arts Council. Coach House Books also acknowledges the support of the Government of Ontario through the Ontario Book Publishing Tax Credit and the Government of Canada through the Book Publishing Industry Development Program.

LIBRARY AND ARCHIVES CANADA
CATALOGUING IN PUBLICATION

Derry, David, 1975-
    Sentimental exorcisms / David Derry.

ISBN 978-1-55245-224-0

    I. Title.

PS8607.E7513S42 2009   C813'.6   C2009-904272-X *for Shannon*

Just Watch:
An Apologia

It was the simple logic of two premises and their inevitable conclusion that ultimately led me to become a voyeur. First, a few feeble acts of missionary sex with my co-operative former girlfriend had numbed me to those pleasures (A_1 becomes B[oring]); escorting her to the door, I reflected on the nature of desire, on all the trifles already discarded by my sensuous and sentimental appetites (other A's had become B). My conclusion, if predictable, was persuasive: attainment is annihilation, is liberation (all A's become B). Rhomboid ruby, pubic crown, that word-bearing wispy crux of a girl – I shut the door behind her, picked up *The Picture of Dorian Gray* and read.

Five or six monastic weeks passed, me burning the midnight oil. As one of the University of Toronto's top English undergrads, living on my own, I was free as an eagle and happy as a lark. I wrote a first-rate essay about Wilde's influence on English Modernism, listened to Schubert, dreamed in heroic terms. Meanwhile, my spurned libido: like the turgid buds loosening in the kind spring sun, dropping pollen on the lawn, it grew – a glance at a time – out from the shadows, as exclusively orificial in its aims as ever, and demanding enactment, yes – but like the writer who requires mere crumbs of the outer realm to feed his creation, I no longer wished to participate.

Oh, my dear girls, you deceptively simple compositions: one stands on the corner, shouldering an attaché case, and by accident exposes her scarlet bra strap; another makes sure nobody's looking before she bends like a beast for a box of condoms on the bottom shelf. I could go on ad nauseam, listing contradictory attitudes, on and on about feminine wiles and their cracks, invaded by jeans that are far too tight, or by a sweaty pair of Spandex short shorts.

Things came to a head in July. A mass of hot American air slammed Toronto on the first of the month, stinking of brewer's yeast and lake sewage, and the streets thronged with thousands of practically naked girls. I bolted myself inside my apartment, tried to keep at my studies like a good responsible son. But the mere click of a female's footfalls past my gaping window and I'd be done for, a wreck, slumped across my desk with no place to go.

A week of air-quality advisories came and went. My books abandoned, I prowled the city in a maze of longing, ratiocination and untested hypotheses. Finally, Saturday morning, lying tangled in my sheet, I deemed my logic sound – i.e., satisfaction effects elimination, so to root out my one irregular vein of sexuality, I simply had to indulge it. And if my plan of action did not exactly qualify as an uncompromising categorical imperative, nor was it simply me mindlessly succumbing to my urges. For the sake of my studies, for my expectant parents who had invested so much in my nebulous future – for the anonymous wife at the centre of that distant nebula – I had to get on with it, to slake my impossible thirst before the thing got away on me and my light summer course load.

You must understand there are few more upstanding than me. It's my conviction that both rapists and wife beaters should be castrated as a matter of course. For I believe in the larger good, the big picture. The need for pragmatic action. 'Minimize harm,' my dad would say. But as so often happens with situational ethics, I was caught on the horns of a dilemma. I hesitated before the ladders, stacked in front of the hardware store, and considered the harm that either action or inaction might entail. By proceeding, I'd clearly be committing deliberate – if hands-off – incursions into people's sacred privacy. But if they didn't realize, was harm done? On the other hand, indefinitely suppressing my desire as best I could, praying that my academic standing wouldn't sink along with my parents' pride, seemed a risky bet. Of course the possibility of being caught red-handed had to be factored into the equation. But so did the common knowledge that an initially quite innocent frustrated desire is often the seed of more sinister tendencies. I weighed a sixteen-foot aluminum ladder and decided it was right.

The cashier, a kitteny teen, managed to evade my smiles. Then her nipples responded instantly to the one downward glance of my flashing gaze. I pictured those nipples all the way home, hard like my resolve. But with an overdue paper on psychosexual symbolism in *The Turn of the Screw* suddenly heavy on my mind, there wasn't time to daydream. I muffled the tops of the ladder rails with old socks and duct tape, stashed the thing in a dilapidated garage behind the building and raced inside for a shower before putting my nose to the grindstone.

Admittedly, certain windows had already caught my passive eye, on my way home from the library late at night, or returning from my friend's (whom I'll call 'Albert'). Once I glimpsed what looked to be flesh; but, despite backtracking and slowly passing a second time, I couldn't ascertain whether it actually was an object of delight. I began taking evening strolls, following alleys behind houses and the peripheries of parks. Such activities sound suspect, certainly, but from my perspective they remained well outside the bounds of voyeurism proper.

That Saturday evening I was completely out of sorts. I phoned Albert, whom I've known since boarding school, but hung up after three rings and angrily searched the freezer for a bite to eat. Cursing, I tried him again, this time letting him answer; finding his voice tedious and slightly enraging, I barked that I was far too busy to play chess and ordered myself a pizza instead.

The vapid television. Gorging on Hawaiian deep-dish, I scanned my umpteen channels over and over until 10:29 on the DVD clock finally became 10:30.

Off with my gym shorts – on with crisp new jeans and a long-sleeved shirt, both black. I looked foolish, somewhere between a friendless wannabe rocker and an unconvincing artiste, nothing like the upright fellow in white or tan khakis and a collared blue shirt I normally present. But the white painter's coveralls (another life: I painted houses the summer between high school and university, with Albert, who by rights should come clean about those filched undies he probably still keeps in a shoebox under his bed) that I pulled overtop seemed a bit more a part of me and certainly gave the right impression. I turned off all the lights and left.

It so happened I'd become aware of the habits of several local households. A young couple, for instance, lived in a house that backed onto the alley behind my building. He was a typical male, egotistical, bent on pornography and computer games, essentially a cipher, while she had a compact, underappreciated little body on her. They usually made for the bedroom shortly after eleven. But that night their house was dark as an unburgled tomb. Helpless as a child, I stood staring at the windows opaquely reflecting the city's jaundiced light.

My second prospect was only four backyards away and housed a large, cumbersome family: three kids, a husband and a wife. She was one I'd seen out walking, long skirts billowing like curtains, and I happily recall her struggle as a pursuant wind kept at her, kept at her substantial, round behind. A television flickered downstairs; above, a half-drawn blind winked a heavy lid over the lighted bedroom window. Setting down the ladder, I penetrated a low border hedge and stole across the lawn, to peer breathlessly inside: children, on the floor, under a blanket, engrossed in the screen. Good enough. I stripped down to black and angled my ladder next to a fir tree.

I started to climb with tentative steps, almost afraid a rung might snap. But those aluminum ladders, with each step they flex, to thrust their climber after grand ideas. I stopped just below the windowsill, knees bent. Blood drummed in my ears, my hands and feet were numb, but nothing could be done for that. I simply tapped the same intrepid resolve with which I used to dive straight into icy water at good old Camp Kamachee and straightened my legs.

Bathos: Greek for *depth*. A shallow-bottomed lake. I banged my figurative head against the following scene: a television at the foot of the bed showed the throes of some bloody chaos; immediately below me lay the flaxen head of my curvaceous doll, sleeping; and the torpid husband beside her was about to lose the glasses off the tip of his whistling schnozz. This signally bleak *tableau 'vivant'* was crowned by a fat brown beagle – of the smelliest sort, I could imagine – laid out between them and gnawing the remote.

I wanted to smash the glass and tear off their sheets! Stifling a scream, I descended the ladder as swiftly as quietly possible and beat a fast retreat across the yard. My only remaining hope lay with the evening's last possibility, an ess-y, svelte black girl.

Tall and lean, she'd kick when she walked, reminding me of a wishbone. I don't remember the short dash to her house, only crossing an empty lot, reassured by the protection it afforded. A room downstairs was bright: there she sat watching TV alone. In the window above, an air conditioner hummed and ticked. I set my ladder beside it and, tucking myself under a lilac, was surprisingly content to lie embowered by the protective bed of night, with a sporadic breeze soughing overhead.

When the downstairs light went out, I scrambled up to the second-highest rung, not generally a safe place to stand, but to keep from being seen I'd have to watch downward through the top pane. She entered – a faint halo caught in her loose evening afro – before I'd even had a chance to adjust myself properly, and was tugging off her clothes, tossing them in the corner as she made a beeline for the bed (to masturbate, I grinningly surmised), forcing me to dodge from sight before the essentials were off. But I cautiously espied her dark arm peeling back the bedspread, a tantalizing prologue, followed at once by a flash of the novel piece that her fine black body was, all that for so long had insinuated itself into my heart from under tight hobble skirts. She switched off the light. I kissed the cold bricks and raced home to flip through some magazines before retiring as well.

One tiny blue tablet, a draught of water: a heavy, satisfied sleep.

A month of twice-weekly expeditions ensued. Mondays and Thursdays were my nights of action. Steadfast abstinence at all other times ensured I went unnoticed and afforded me a sense of self-restraint. My spare hours I spent artistically detailing a map of the neighbourhood, soon to cover an entire bedroom wall, and also monkeying around with a branching agenda.

My first conclusion: most people's lives are boring. A couple of unusual encounters aside, I'm not exaggerating in saying that three quarters of the couples I tracked led unremarkable – virtually non-existent – sex lives. I blame the flaccid husbands. True, women reach their prime long after men are spent, but even the youngest bucks behaved like neuters. I quickly learned that if I was to have any hope of vanquishing my overweening desire, I'd need to expand my territory.

In accordance with the first rule of strategic planning, I

took to my desk and prioritized. Intellectual honesty was indispensable, as well as a willingness to sacrifice certain secondary attractions. After much typing and deleting, probing myself from every angle, I cleared the screen and with deliberate keystrokes distilled the spirit of my lust into three main objectives: 1. Observation of lesbians; 2. Observation of a Chinese girl fornicating; 3. Observation of a woman being sodomized. It seemed to me that by witnessing these scenarios I'd exhaust my spectator's desire and – sated, bored and happy – could revert to an orthodox lifestyle.

It's incredible what one can accomplish if one puts one's mind to it. My parents used to tell me that, but I never gave it much thought. Objectives 1 and 2 were notched in my belt, so to speak, within a month of conception. Just as my parents counselled, it took patience, discipline and an open mind.

First, I dropped my summer courses. That a couple of poor grades should tarnish my transcript, perhaps preventing me from graduating with distinction, all because of a fleeting distraction, was absurd. Better to concentrate on the task at hand and re-enrol in September, refreshed for my final year. Thus relieved of obligations, I deepened my commitment, exploring promising neighbourhoods during the day – Chinatown, the University District, Gaytown – and returning at night to climb and shimmy, quick with great expectations.

I witnessed a lot that harried month, acts that surprised and disgusted me. But I'm not writing pornography, so only two notes are germane to the present discussion: 1. I did taste success, 66.6 percent to be exact, inadequate but sufficient to prove my father's sententious counsel sound: 'Accomplishment is a triune consummation of vision, imagination and application!' – an aphorism he'd pen inside the cover of my daily planner at the beginning of each new school year. 2. Objective 3 was the 33.3 percent I sorely missed.

The male body is repulsive. It serves the crude, if necessary, role of penetrator, in itself best ignored. No, my drive to Sodom was not by the high road of homoerotic transposition. I simply asterisked the act for its guttural moan. In the fourth month of that four-month relationship with my former girlfriend, one attempt at sodomy had transpired. I'd been feeling tongue-tied, disinclined to discuss things; eventually she wheedled it out of me, smiled and said, 'Why not?'

She knelt on the bed – I nudged in behind her. Then balked, just an inch from that fetid hole.

How stupid we looked, hunched like that. My affection for her vanished, like a wisely deleted simile, but the asterisk of the act would soon wink again in the heavens of my mind. Objective 3 was to be the acme and the omega of my illicit pursuits.

A methodical approach seemed impossible. How to recognize a female sodomite? I wasted three weeks on random chance, hitting downtown neighbourhoods without the ladder, stooping to have a look through edges of imperfectly blinded basement windows. My initial groundless optimism quickly succumbed to rage and despair.

One night, walking up Yonge Street, yet again I was questioning whether my plan was realistic. Already it was the end of August, a Sunday, very late, and a diffuse flow of traffic was moving north. I'd gotten stuck leapfrogging with a crew of garbage collectors who kept squealing to a stop immediately in front of me, shooting bags into the back end of their dripping truck and then roaring forth to stop ahead of me again. In the middle of navigating one especially fouled section of pavement, I was startled by a dainty hand brandishing a whip.

Whap! Whap! I froze, credulous from exhaustion. No. Just a storefront dummy. Delectably attired but utterly inert. Still, I kept staring, pondering the curve of her buttocks, the cleft in her groin, reluctant to go trudging off home with nothing to show for my effort.

But hold on – a sex shop. Why hadn't I thought of that? *Loraine's Palace*, read the extinguished neon sign, in cursive script, punctuated with an exclamatory cat-o'-nine-tails! I chuckled, sort of to the mannequin, sort of to myself, until my reflection caught my eye. No matter – I knew where I was and would be back. A bounce to my step, I marched home and popped three sleeping pills for good measure.

It's important to remember I was harming no one. On the spectrum of illicit activities, mine falls at the fringe, in the light-grey zone where social impropriety gets called criminal. The crimes that are black, the truly vicious acts, have consequences so immediate they offer no real temptation to the man with a conscience. But nobody was harmed by my behaviour – I repeat, no one was really affected. Of what am I to repent then? To whom do I address this defence of my struggle for self-improvement?

Soon I was a regular. Larry, the polite Chinese man who owned the place, would smile and nod discreetly when I entered. This quiet familiarity was reassuring, if a little embarrassing. Incidentally, Larry was heavy and poorly groomed. I can still see him, stuffed behind the counter in a sweat suit, lifting gleaming noodles to his mouth, immured in unshelved stock. In my hand I have a video, *Lucy's Hunger*; Larry sets down his dinner box and chopsticks and, unmoved by gaping Lucy, checks the price. 'Twenty-fo ninety.' He slips the video into a brown paper bag and – 'Sank you' – hands it back with a complaisant nod. That's how I remember him, and each time I do, his hair and the noodles gleam a bit more brilliantly and the number of dildos peering out from half-unpacked boxes seems to grow.

Of course a video can come in handy, or magazines; the dildo and Ben-Wa balls were a waste of money (I told taciturn Larry they were for my girlfriend). But being a regular, paying customer made it possible for me to snoop.

Too bad the clientele was mostly male. The races were all present, the classes fairly counted. Now and then a pair of jocular fags slipped in or snickering adolescents had to be chased out, but most of us entered alone, browsed alone and eventually exited nervously. The rare girl that did appear was always armed with a circumspect meathead.

What kept me faithful to Larry? 1. My superstition that an Invisible Hand was behind the one with the whip; and, more importantly, 2. Mother's trenchant advice: 'Patience is the ingredient missing from unrealized dreams. Choose your noble path and see it through.' This complement to my father's maxim consoled me through fruitless, thrice-weekly snoops. From the moment of arriving I'd want out, but when my ninety minutes were up, I wouldn't want to leave. What else was there to do? I had postponed re-enrolling in school. Still, I exercised restraint, determined not to lose sight of myself, and also concerned with appearances.

Two weeks into this new routine, fractured dreams started breaking into the hitherto impenetrable darkness of my pharmaceutical sleeps. I dreamed of myself as a child, so it seemed – but I was an adult, I think – feeling around for a crack in the boarding-school wall that I used for hiding recreational drugs from the housemasters. Somehow, I accidentally took some LSD, in the car, on my way home with my parents. The bare-branched trees were flashing past, my parents' eyes sharply lashing. And I got mired in such viscous space that I couldn't even roll down the window.

I awoke to the growing conviction that my real life was being lived in a most occluded place.

There's a sense of right and wrong behind even our most wanton behaviour. Especially our most wanton behaviour. I report this not because I was assailed by shame (although sometimes I was, it is true, particularly when noon hour's vacuous light struck my dreadful dreams flat across the pavement of another afternoon), but because my ongoing reading and reflection has shown me some interesting correspondences between my erotic objectives and the Victorian mores I descend from. For instance, in *Confessions of a White Slaver*, by the reformed Peregrine Samuels, circa 1897, we read, 'Oriental concupiscence, *incurable in the yellow races*, is aggravated by the widespread use of opium by Chinese of both sexes, whereby some of the blame lies at the feet of our unscrupulous foreign office.' Another rare find: the once illicit *Physiology of Unnatural Acts* (1882), which devotes entire (tastefully illustrated) chapters to both 'The Gomorran Maidservant' and 'Unnatural Intercourse among the French.' Like subliminal messages in TV commercials, my forefathers' moralistic prurience had been transmitted to me.

Back to Larry's and the final stage in this quest for resolution. On Friday of the fourth week of September, a peroxide blond entered on stiletto heels, sporting leather pants and a cropped black top. She came with a greasy man. Around her eyes and corrugating her upper lip, lines betrayed an aging contradicted by an apparent firmness of rump. The pair surveyed a rack of sex toys, cackling conspiratorially about this one and that, and I thought of her leathers as skin, as the rind around a somewhat desiccated orange that, with effort, one might still manage to peel. Suddenly, and with a very casual attitude, she took down a thick pink butt plug and snickered. They passed it back and forth, until eventually she did put it back, but almost reluctantly, certainly slowly enough for it to be inferred that she was not averse to the business for which it had been manufactured. I waited for them to leave.

Now. I thrust several magazines at Larry, saying I'd be back, and rushed out the door. North. I was with them in seconds and, reassured, drifted back a bit in the early-evening crowd.

As we walked, I wondered, Will they drive? I was alert for cabs. What if they go to a movie? Or a strip club? Should I enter or wait outside? What about a bar?

We descended into the subway and, on a train north, positioned ourselves at opposite ends of the same car, which was packed and stunk of human. I couldn't see her, but he was tall enough for me to keep tabs on his thin, dancing ponytail, until it swished and slunk toward the door when we clattered into Bloor Station. I followed suit. We descended further underground and caught an eastbound train, full like the other. Half the passengers disembarked at Broadview. He took a seat beside her, right close together, her leather juncture, his hairy hand, fumbling, straying – dammit, what's hidden before our eyes! The train screamed into Coxwell, and we all leaned as one against the braking speed, then popped erect.

Above ground it was already getting dusky. Although we'd been sweating out an Indian summer, the air smelt like fall, and I distinctly remember having to banish from my mind my mother's wistful pronouncement of the season's end ('So short – so short, the summer of life.'). Two blocks west on Danforth, they turned into a doorway beside a picture-frame shop, in a two-storey brick affair, an arrangement common in that part of the city: stores below, apartments on top, backed by a laneway. I zipped down the driveway to the back and, concealing myself beneath a crab apple heavy with overripe fruit, focused on the upstairs windows.

First, a light toward the front: the hall. Next, a small frosted window implied a bathroom. Was she urinating? No, there she was in the kitchen, pulling out some pots, beyond a sliding glass door that opened onto a deck and fire escape. Behind her passed the man to a room out front ... a room, it occurred to me, that could only face the street. The bedroom. No other window faced the back. The bedroom faced the street.

Stumbling into the darkening driveway that led to Danforth, I propped my crestfallen person against a wall, sickened by the thought that there was no end in sight, when a splash of weak light appeared on the pavement before me.

Oh, benevolent spirits! Mine slipped from its chains of despair to flit and flicker far past a small second-storey window directly above me and commune with the minions of high hope that dwell in a darkening firmament. I had no doubts about that lighted square, like Pascal and his bush.

Granted, circumstances were treacherous: I'd have to use my ladder; there'd be passersby in the street; a car could wheel in at any moment. But desperation and an inordinate capacity for misplaced optimism allow us to rationalize possibilities that prudence should preclude. The driveway would soon be dark; I could lean my ladder almost parallel to the wall; people avoid alleys at night.

Back to the crab apple. She was chopping a cabbage; several tins sat open on the counter. I ran out to the street and flagged a cab.

Already half-changed into my blacks and whites, I phoned Albert to borrow his car, explaining that a friend he'd never met was moving to town and I'd agreed to help paint his apartment. He sounded annoyed, interrogated me about this new friend of mine and about what I'd been up to. But he did consent. Twenty minutes later I strapped my ladder to his station wagon, with a promise that I'd play chess soon.

It was good and dark. The radio was tuned to some kind of electronica, as if I wasn't charged up enough already, but its relentless beat did nicely underlie my determination, drove me fast past female freshmen on Bloor, over the bridge and the valley below. In the theatre of my mind, a single loop of hope: the coveted moment of penetration.

I parked a safe distance from 'the scene of the crime,' on a street east of Coxwell, and, in an effort to seem harmless, loosened my gait and relaxed my mouth, hurrying through the backstreets, emerging onto Danforth only fifty metres from my dangerous point of access. At the driveway I betrayed no hesitation, just turned in, and the anxiety that in truth had been threatening to fell me noticeably diminished at the sight of a luminous slit between drawn curtains in the window upstairs. I ran to the comforting tree.

Kitchen light, on. Hallway and bathroom, both dark. Nobody in sight. No time to lose. I stripped off my coveralls and stuffed them in the crook of a branch. A raucous clutch of teens lurched past the end of the driveway. Would they have noticed, I soberly asked myself, had I been in place? 'Drunkenness of the citizenry' got added to the list of propitious conditions that had convinced me of my plan's infallibility. I took my ladder and set it at a steep angle without so much as a tap.

I have no idea whether anyone passed while I was at work. With my footing secure, the job was done. All I could do was climb.

One rung at a time, don't rush. Descending is more treacherous than ascending. I always felt stronger the further I pulled from the ground.

In my mind's eye, my face is right next to a window with burgundy curtains and a crack where they meet. One hand grips a rung, the other's on the sill, and I tingle like I'm conducting a weak electric charge. In there I hear it, that pained mantra of lust. But can't see. I shift a little; shift a little more. Still nothing but whimpers and groans. Never mind, try to enjoy. I go a rung higher. There, there, I hear her, the frantic animal attempting its escape. Dammit, I need to see.

'What are you doing?' I froze. 'Bitch ...' I couldn't see. Something crashed. 'Get back over here, you little bitch.' A shriek was clapped right off. 'Over here.' Grunt. Now her: 'Get off, no ... stop it, uh, stop ...' *Bang! Bang!* Shots?

'Jesus, Van, change the channel.' Huh? 'And open the curtains while you're at it. It's scorching in here.'

When you set your ladder steep, like I did, every move must oppose a potential topple. One lurching step down, that's it, and every bloody organ knew that I'd forgotten. My clutching form traced an arc across the driveway and crashed against the opposite wall. I was dangling from a shuddering rung.

'What the fuck?': the sum of his irate response. Hand over hand, I started to descend the ladder.

'Angie! Call the cops.'

I released my grip.

Pulling myself together, heading for the street – but I stopped, fearing witnesses, and ran for the back. That was my mistake, the flip of the coin I regret to this day. For as I rounded the building, my would-be captor came booming down the fire escape like a runaway orangutan and tackled me. I landed and curled, anticipating blows, but there came only hot breath in my ear: 'What the fuck? What the fuck!' We waited in the dirt without another word.

The cops arrived with their invasive lights and noise. I was cuffed and pulled upright. 'Mr. Barrett,' they said, 'Mr. Barrett.' They pushed my wallet back into my pants. Aggravating my misery, the sounds I'd taken to be wind-stirred leaves while down on the ground were in fact the whispers of two or three clusters of onlookers who hung back and stared. Besides the policeman's grip steering me by the arm to one of the cruisers, a distinct sensation of thumbs stays with me. Being pressed down by thumbs. The shake of a bathrobed grandmother's puffy head; the policemen's unrelenting, mechanical use of my surname from handcuffing to fingerprinting – despite the harmless nature of a transgression that still feels more on the order of a finger caught in the cookie dough than a bona fide crime.

My careful logic is dismissed out of hand. Justifications prompt cries from my mother, and Dad's angry fist, planted on the kitchen counter. Only my magnanimous lawyer treats me like myself, although he maintains the futility of this defence and keeps reiterating the practical need for me to repent.

Van struck me to the ground – the jig was up; a cop pressed on my head to get me into the car, like he was recorking a bottle of wine; someone in the crowd yelled, 'Pervert': society in action.

Was it worth it? The question is unanswerable, as in any failed endeavour. True, I've lost everything I was trying to save with my bold manoeuvring. I'm living with my parents, whose pride in me is gone, and I'm temporarily suspended from the Department. My hypothesis has been neither proven nor irrefutably disproved. My hunger's not quite sated. But when it seems in life that you have a fighting chance of conquering some problematic aspect of yourself, if you don't take it you end up with not only the original problem, still compounding, but also with regret. It's enough to make an effort, I believe that. To give it your all and walk away a loser.

Driving home from the police station, with the windows shut tight, my parents wouldn't stop eyeing me in the rear-view mirror – until my mother, unable to contain herself a moment longer, twisted around and asked, in her anguished tone, 'What *are* we without our morals?'

Can you understand my answer, that there's no way to know?

ॐ

Semicolon, Coma, Full Stop:
A Treatise on Punctuation

'And, be it noted, the crime is committed solely by the punctuation; a perfectly normal sentence has been ruthlessly hacked into three bits, with the result that one bit still lives and the other two are cut off in their prime.' [1]

No Sinclair arrived on the anticipated train. The sentence of disembarking passengers ended in a four-point ellipsis of three wheelchair travellers and a crying little boy. But I didn't bother calling Marjory, my grey-maned wife of so many years. I knew there'd be no message from Sinclair. Instead I sighed and returned to the bench at the base of a Corinthian column to cross and recross my legs while watching passersby reading names of Canadian cities off the high frieze inside Union Station. That was the end of April 2002, some forty-three years too late, some seven months too early, and I dearly wished he wasn't coming.

'Sinclair here.'

My heart sank like an anchor and I gripped the phone.

Silence, a suck of breath, before his gravelly voice intoned, 'Te′di:?'[2]

'Sinclair. Jesus, Sinclair. Where are you?'

'In Montreal, where I've been all along. Where are you?'

'I mean, my goodness, what … ?'

Many times I'd found myself constipated in his presence, literally and linguistically. I never quite understood what he wanted. But he charmed me with that quicksilver tongue and his praise for my sophomoric poetry. Below is the piece that prompted him to phone me in 1958, after it had been published in the student paper.

---

1 G. V. Carey, *Mind the Stop: A Brief Guide to Punctuation.* 2nd ed. (Middlesex: Penguin Books, 1958), 14.

2 Thus transcribed according to the International Phonetic Alphabet (IPA), to be accented like 'ta-*dah*,' main stress on second syllable: Sinclair's purpose in this Frenchifying wrench was never entirely clear.

The Closest Man

The men close to me
cross the street
baring wide-tooth grimace.
Do not confuse them for a smile.

Your teeth, bedded
with gold, are fine
insurance in a miserable time.

Otherwise,
delight at the crematorium.

I admit I was quite proud of it. And Sinclair had a ponderous voice that tended to drum up bold possibilities: 'Te´di:' – I swear he pronounced it like that from the first – 'let me be your cremator.'

I cleared my throat. 'Who is this?'

'I see some silver. Now let's make it shine.'

I hadn't a clue what that riddler was getting at and very nearly hung up.

'The name's Sinclair.' He paused long enough to make me uneasy. 'I'm a poet and I think we should meet. You've got something that wants polishing.'

Needless to say, I opened like a dewy morning glory, gushing into the phone. I said *when* and *wherefore* and then strutted about my dorm room conducting interviews with myself, pontificating on the significance of verse, disparaging my peers. But my confidence dissolved in front of the mirror. For at twenty-four I looked like a fourteen-year-old. At fourteen I had looked nine. I was a virgin, frightfully ashamed of my puniness, and the residence's communal bathroom had so terrorized me I was wont to scribble at my desk into the darkest hours simply to be able to shower in private.

And Sinclair was a man. He seemed so from day one, his knuckles sprouting hair like crabgrass, his swarthy damascene face and that head of tangled black curls that withstood so much passionate tugging as he pored over my poems with an intrusive pen. Now try to imagine my small head with its covering of fine blond hair. From a block away, from two, from three, from four, from five, he'd be watching me approach him at the Irish pub where he spent most of that summer; I'd shrink and lengthen my stride. Or take November, when we sat on a park bench and he wore a spicy grey sweater so heavy it hangs over my memory like chain mail, and the first shivers of the season's snow spun curlicues across the page we were working on together.

Marjory loitered in the kitchen until I hung up the phone. 'Who was that, Ted?'

Gripping the counter, I stared out the window at the budded drooping branchlets of our weeping willow.

'Ted?'

'I'm sorry?'

'Who were you talking to?'

Ridiculously, I felt unable to answer, and gaped at her contracting, corrugated brow. 'Um, an old fr–, or sort of acq–' I stumbled to a kitchen chair and must have looked ill, because next thing I knew her cold hand was patting my forehead. 'Could you get me some water please?'

She brought it. 'But what's the matter?'

'Nothing.' I gulped from the glass, abruptly stood and took it to the sink. 'Everything's fine, why?'

'Well, who *was* that?'

'Nobody, just a guy I knew in university, before we met. Sinclair.' I grinned foolishly. 'I really have to go to the bathroom.' I hurried downstairs to the basement and called up to her, 'He's coming to Toronto for a literary conference, so I said he could stay with us, okay?'

Her hard-soled slippers came pattering down after me and she said through the bathroom door, 'Pardon?'

'He needs a place to stay and I said he could stay here.'

I sat waiting for a response, but when none came, flushed and emerged to find her frowning on the couch.

'Thanks.'

'What was I supposed to say? He asked.'

'I've never even heard of this person before.' Her mouth tightened into a knot. 'For how long?'

'A couple of days.' In fact I hadn't had the presence of mind to ask. 'Three at the most.'

She flipped her hand dismissively, picked up the remote and absented herself by turning on the television. 'I guess you'd better clear out the guest room,' she said as I slunk up the stairs.

The 'guest room' has been my bedroom for at least a decade – my bedroom and so much more: it's my office, my comfort, my window on the fertile smells that waft up from the garden in spring. Two years ago I retired from Robarts Library at the University of Toronto, but my job in Cataloguing had long ceased to bring me pleasure, so no attendant crisis occurred. If memory serves, I was at that time in the thick of an essay tracking the several waves of Latinate arrivals in the English language. The tract, some 25,000 words, was written in Modern English but with a shifting lexicon that reflected the resources available to the various periods under discussion. I remember the lilacs were in late bloom and beginning to rot, and Marjory made a special goulash to celebrate my super-annuation, which fell just a month after hers. But the entire time we were eating and cleaning the dishes and taking a turn in the garden, all I could think about was the soft evening light I was missing in my hideaway. When finally I sat down at my desk with a mint tea and tugged the chain on my jade-shaded lamp, dusk was over, I'd missed it all and my monograph wouldn't console me.

I assuaged my disappointment by picking through papers, pruning out those that pertained to my former employment, and a few hours later I dropped two full bags into the battered steel garbage pails at the side of the house, firm that nothing unpleasant would ever enter the guest room again.

Now I was about to introduce Sinclair, like an invasive weed, into my bower?

The next train from Montreal was scheduled to arrive shortly before three. I stood up from the bench, stretched, walked to the bathroom and examined my smooth pink face in the mirror. If only I'd retained a head of hair. 'If I angle myself just so, perhaps I look a bit sophisticated?' But who actually believes their own posturing? We wouldn't do it if we did. I tossed a crumpled paper towel in the trash, planted my black felt cap firmly on my head and hurried downstairs to Arrivals.

I was not optimistic. Sinclair scorned punctuality. Not only was he late as a matter of course, he had for a while convinced me that my own routine timeliness was yet another aspect of the 'spiritual suicide' from which he was determined to save me. I watched the First Class passengers file in from the platform and contrasted each passing face with my mental image of Sinclair, retouching the latter accordingly: age-enhancing, bronzing, blanching, bespectacling, balding, bearding, inflating, emaciating, gentrifying, dissipating by transplanting a tumid nose. Several times I had to abort a wave or dissemble a smile when my cautious gesture was met with indifference or outright hostility. My First Class effort ended fruitlessly. Next came Economy Class and I hadn't a chance, the crowd was too thick. My gaze, with its uncertain aim, moved from stout to beetle-browed to gaunt to womanly, reverse, repeat, include, and finally abruptly and hopelessly ended on a fellow bent over his walker. I returned my attention to a clutch of men and women who had halted and formed a circle around their luggage not far from the platform exit. They cast worried looks in all directions, and periodically the men conferred and sent an envoy down the hall. I sidled toward them pessimistically, anticipating a third sentence on the bench, when an electrifying gurgle shocked me from behind: 'Te´di:!' The hairs on my neck erected.

I turned around. 'Sinclair?'

'Te´di:, over here. Give me a hand over here with my bags.' That walkered old man was calling to me with what was either a grimace or a smile.

'Sinclair?' His face – once a concord of cheeky exclamations, well-anchored frowns and sympathetic tildes across the brow – now brought to mind the early draft of an essay, so densely slashed and overwritten only the author can make any sense of it. Two tan Gladstones bracketed his feet. Slowly I approached, smiling anxiously, trying to reconcile, in the fifteen steps between us, my well-preserved mental portrait with this inverted Dorian Gray.

'Sinclair!'

We embraced. He smelled the same.

'You've brought a lot of luggage.'

'Yes, will you carry them for me? This damn walker.' He glared at the bags.

I tried to pick one up. 'What's in here?'

'Some books and things.'

'I'd better take one at a time. My heart's not what it once was.'

He muttered something about 'years ago,' which ruffled my feathers.

'Punctual' and 'punctuate' both derive from the Latin *pūnctum*, 'point,' past participle of *pungere*, 'sting, pierce, puncture, prick' (from the hypothetical Indo-European base, *peug-*, whence *pūgnus*, 'fist').[3] Similarly, 'impugn': attack by arguments; 'repugn': resist; 'expugn': take by storm; furthermore, 'puncture,' 'pungent,' 'poignant,' 'repugnance,' 'compunction,' 'disappointment' and 'expunge.' All derived from a single word, with no remembered meaning, in our long-lost mother tongue.

When Sinclair phoned me out of the blue, my thoughts were split between some final amendments to an essay on changing usage of the subjunctive mood in Modern English[4] and inchoate plans for an essay on punctuation. By the time he arrived, five days later, I had narrowed down my interest to the semicolon.

This little latecomer has been a source of quite some confusion. The literature variously puts the date of its appearance at 'the 1530s,'[5] 1501[6] and 1494[7]. The first two sources are wrong. M. B. Parkes, the third source, reports the mark was probably invented by the Venetian printer Aldus Manutius the Elder, or

---

3 Ernest Klein, *A Comprehensive Etymological Dictionary of the English Language, Dealing with the origins of words and their sense development thus illustrating the history of civilization and culture* (Amsterdam: Elsevier, 1971), 602.

4 Ted Johnson, 'As It Were,' *Inheriting Fire: The Journal of the Society of Unaligned English Philologists*, 76 (2003): 214–19. In this article I simultaneously discuss and demonstrate the evolving subjunctive. The editors accepted it on the basis of both its 'imaginative format' and 'novel, if speculative, insight.'

5 John McDermott, *Punctuation for Now* (London: Macmillan, 1990), 16.

6 David Chestworth, *Pointing the Way* (London: Cornucopia, 1957), 42.

7 M. B. Parkes, *Pause and Effect: Punctuation in the West* (Aldershot: Scolar Press, 1992), 49.

by someone in his Humanist circle, as a morphological hybrid of the comma and colon and a functional intermediary (punctuation at that time serving a role more elocutionary and rhythmical than grammatical). But one wonders if it might not be so easy. *Not* because of some obscure connection between the semicolon and a similar-looking mark that, in the eighth century, was introduced by copyists into Greek manuscripts to signify interrogation. This damn coincidence has put more than one enthusiast on a false scent over the centuries. In 1785 Joseph Robertson guessed that by morphological inversion, 'placing the comma above the period in this manner and giving it a little curve toward the right hand, at the bottom,' the so-called Greek question mark had been transformed into our question mark;[8] more speculative yet, in 1920 Frederick Hamilton asserted that the Aldine circle had taken the semicolon directly from the Greek grammarians and simply changed its meaning.[9] Once and for all, *no credible evidence points to any connection between this Greek curiosity and Western punctuation.*

I question Parkes' tidy scenario because a mark the same as our semicolon occasionally appears in High Middle Age liturgical manuscripts, used interchangeably with '.' for *punctus versus* or period.[10] I hypothesize an evolution of the semicolon's function between the fourteenth and sixteenth centuries, resulting in the mark that Aldus the Elder eventually systematized and disseminated (thanks largely to his overwhelmingly popular 'Old Roman' letter font).

---

8 Joseph Robertson, *An Essay on Punctuation* (London: J. Walter, 1785), 13.

9 Frederick W. Hamilton, *Punctuation: A Primer of Information About the Marks of Punctuation and Their Use Both Grammatically and Typographically* (Chicago: Committee on Education, United Typothetae of America, 1920), 4.

10 Peter Clemoes, *Occasional Papers, Number 1: Liturgical Influence on Late Old English and Early Middle English Punctuation* (Binghamton: Center for Medieval and Renaissance Studies, State University of New York, 1952), 6.

I longed to say all this and more to Sinclair on our way home from the station. I was exploding with information. But if I knew Sinclair, he'd regard my project with scorn. And so we drove in silence, like two men who must shortly set about a potentially fatal task, like clearing land mines.

'I'm looking forward to introducing you to Marjory.'

'Who?'

'Marjory, my wife.'

'Didn't know you had a wife.'

'Going on forty-two years.' In fact I'd met her the night after Sinclair had fled London (Ontario) for Montreal, with a final curse hurled up at my latched window. Against my better judgment, but desperate for respite from my conflicting thoughts and feelings and with nothing else to do, I'd gone alone to a poetry reading. There were no empty tables, but I noticed her, alone as well, trembling in votive candlelight in the corner. Tapping the quickly dwindling trickle of courage that Sinclair had fought to instill in me, I stole across the room and asked to join her. We were married within the year. That was the last poetry reading either of us ever attended.

He was scrutinizing me.

I pulled into the driveway and turned off the ignition. 'And this is our home.'

Our home's a modest house in the east end of Toronto, north of Danforth and east of Broadview. A storey-and-a-half, it has a small front lawn, a driveway down the side to the garage and a sizable yard with lilacs, a pear tree, two apples, Marjory's flowers and vegetable garden, and the willow right at the back. We moved here in 1965.

Marjory opened the door and stood looking down at the car with that irritating affectation of a smile that she inherited from her mother, which resembles an expression of horror and fools none.

Marjory and I have sustained a surprisingly sturdy rapport that some might call dispassionate but to me is realistic. We're shy, restrained people who don't ask for much besides a little peace and comfort. Compared with my parents, whose relationship might be described as pacifically seething, or with Marjory's father, a mildly abusive alcoholic, and her mother, a meek woman about whom I don't remember much – compared with either of these couples I'd say we've been rather successful. But Sinclair was always an idealist, especially when it came to me and relationships.

I was in my final year of Honours English at the University of Western Ontario when he took me under his wing. I had had only two dates in my life: a blind one (I first understood that the spine's our ground, our emotional lightning rod, when struck by her split second of naked disappointment as she opened the door); and later, a prayer-weighted dinner and drive-in with a quiet stranger from my Victorian Literature class. The latter unravelled more or less as follows: stilted dinner conversation about studies, siblings (or lack thereof in my case), favourite colours and songs; then came the movie, with Rock Hudson, and I sat paralyzed. Driving back to Spencer Hall I made a white-knuckled request to go steady to the windshield, which she rejected, kindly touching my shoulder. I dropped her off and that was that, I withdrew from Victorian Literature on Monday.

But Sinclair held some sway on campus – for certain crowds he was an enigma. In year two of his doctorate a conflict with the chair of the English Department had resulted in his abandoning it for full-time employment at a bookstore where, unbeknownst to me, all the student poets hung around. So, not long after he had impressed on me his seal of approval, I found myself courted by a morose freshman obsessed with Sartre, which returns us to Sinclair's idealism – his volatile intolerance, I should say. One noon hour he stumbled upon us in a restaurant downtown. Yvonne was telling me that Sartre had got it right, that the sole object of absurd, gnarled life was cancerous expansion. Sinclair arrived just as she said, 'The world is crushing me up against myself.' Having not read the existentialists, I nodded obligingly, and shortly she left for class.

Sinclair railed at me: 'What was that? Why didn't you say anything?'

'Pardon?'

'She's a bullshitter, a baby.'

'How do you mean?'

He pinned my hand down with his great mitt. 'That depressive little kitten's a fraud and you know it. She's bored. Her despair's manufactured so she can smoke with a pout.'

'Well, I haven't read –'

'Oh, come on. Have some faith in yourself, Te´di:. You don't believe what you know.' He pressed down harder on my hand. 'You don't even know what you know.'

You see, he was hostile to anyone else's stage of development or level of comfort: 'What are you talking about? You're not saying anything. Simpleton!' It was just an innocent comment. Or else, 'Ho-hum, nobody gives a shit about your confusion. That has nothing to do with poetry.' He'd rip it up.

'The poet is a thief of fire,' he said, having wrapped his arm around my shoulder (that massive black wool coat he always wore in winter). 'Rimbaud.' He handed me a battered copy of *Illuminations* (*A Season in Hell* might have been more appropriate). 'Put this under your pillow and when you get a kink in your neck, read it.'

'One of the symbo– ' I started saying, but he put his hand over my mouth.

'You're only comfortable starving. You tell yourself that there are no feasts to attend, that joy is a lie. But you're wrong. You just need to trust your appetite.' He walked away.

That night at four o'clock in the morning I read from a dog-eared page:

> Pitiful brother! what frightful nights I owed him! 'I have not put enough ardor into this enterprise. I have trifled with his infirmity. My fault should we go back to exile, and to slavery.' He implied I was unlucky and of a very strange innocence, and would add disquieting reasons.[11]

Some sparrows chirped in the birch outside my window even though it was dark as sin.

Marjory watched me helping Sinclair. I set his walker in front of him, and as he stamped, shuffled, wheezed up the walkway and stopped to catch his breath, I hefted his Gladstones into the front hallway. At the bottom of the five steps up to the landing I took his arm and Marjory made to take the other, but Sinclair – I explained later that he'd been out of breath and had intended no rudeness – croaked, 'Stay away, Miriam, I've got Te´di:'s arm.' There was something jocular in it, but she chilled perceptibly.

Until that very morning every flat surface of the guest room, except the unmade bed, had been littered with miscellaneous notes, photocopies, Post-its and a reprint of the famous and anonymous *A TREATISE of Stops, Points, or Pauses, And of Notes which are used in WRITING and in PRINT; Both very neceffary to be well known, And the Ufe of each to be carefully taught. Composed for the Authors Ufe, who is a hearty wel-willer (and accordingly hath endeavoured the promoting of) the*

11 Arthur Rimbaud, 'Vagabonds,' *Illuminations*, 2nd ed., trans. Louise Varèse (New York: New Directions, 1957), 65.

attainments of Children, and others, in the tru Spelling, and exact
Reading of Englifh (self-published in 1680, the first English
work devoted exclusively to punctuation). But I'd boxed my
seminal project and transferred it to the basement, where I
found some books of poetry, to be dusted off and arranged
upstairs. For a bookend I used a heavy brass Prometheus in
mid-evisceration that's been floating around the house forever.

Sinclair entered with a grunt of appreciation.

I hurried back down to fetch his things.

Marjory stood beside them, pressing her perpetually blue
hands to the lukewarm radiator. I grabbed one suitcase, hefted
it upstairs and returned for the other. Now she followed softly
behind me to mill outside the door. Sinclair already had one
bag jerked wide open on the bed, packed with socks, underwear
and books.

He jabbed a thumb at Prometheus. 'I got you that.'

'No, you didn't.'

'Yup. When we were in Chicago that week.'

'Not true, Sinclair. It came from a garage sale, didn't it,
Marjory?'

'What?'

'Didn't I find that bookend at a garage sale?'

'How should I know?'

'Bullshit,' said Sinclair. 'Well, will you move those? Those
books. I gotta put mine somewhere.'

Marjory bobbed her head into the doorway. 'You seem to
have brought an awful lot for a two-day conference.'

'What's that?' He looked at me. 'What did she say? I don't
hear ladies' high-pitched voices very well.'

'She said you seem to have brought quite a bit of stuff
with you.'

'Oh.' He kept piling his books on the bed. He unwrapped a
brass urn. 'Put this on the shelf for me, will you, Te´di:?'

I didn't dare look at Marjory and began making room for it. Her footstamps were dampened by our carpeted stairs, but the door to the backyard crashed like it was inside me.

Sinclair suddenly stopped unpacking and made me sit down beside him on the bed. 'So when did you marry *her*?'

'I told you, over forty years ago.'

He gave that quick, baffled shake of head that always used to shame me. 'Should've guessed.'

I smiled weakly. Any words I might have ventured in our defence were precisely the ones he was implying.

Nothing's changed, I reflected a few minutes later, as I hurried down to look for Marjory: the affectionate archness, his irascible brows. Everything about him made me sick.

I found her raking out the flower beds, her ponytail dancing nervously. I produced some casual remark – grass greening, crocuses past their prime, something to that effect – and she spun round like a soldier, planting the rake handle in the ground so that its vibrating teeth menaced my composure, and waited for me to say something further.

'He's settling in nicely up there.'

'So I noticed.'

'Sorry about this, dear. We'll hardly notice him. He's quite weak.'

'How long is he planning on staying?'

'Just for the literary conference. A couple of days probably.'

She snorted. 'It doesn't look that way to me.'

I nodded in commiseration.

'Who is he again?'

'I told you, a friend from university.'

'You've never even mentioned him before.'

'We knew each other for a year or so, before I met you. Then we just kind of parted,' I said, demonstrating with my hands, and quickly added, ' … when he had to move to Montreal. For work.'

She returned to her aggressive raking but, without turning back to face me, said, 'I don't have the energy for an invalid, Ted. Not at this stage in my life. We took in your mother, we dealt with my parents. Take, take, take. He reminds me of my father.'

'Calm, Marjory. You're getting way ahead of yourself.'

'All those books, and the sweaters! You saw how he treated me. Did you say anything?'

I murmured that of course I would, but after all, he was staying for only a few days. I left her in the garden and went to see if there were any boxes in the garage for my books and the statuette.

Marjory's got the patience of a saint. But is it really patience? I think what drew me to her, besides the simple fact that I found her approachable, was knowing in my heart that she wouldn't ask for much. She, like me, was desirous of companionship, a home with a garden, a place to rest. We're continually told that to be authentically alive you must ask for a lot. I'm not talking about advertisements – I'm talking about impatience and adventurous spirits, the incessant need to take life by the horns. I'm referring to the demands of needlessly ramifying appetites and to the grossly inflated heart. Marjory and I tacitly understood that these were suffering and a trap, that shelter is the thing worth struggling for.

'Let Sinclair keep his barbed verse,' I groaned into my pillow, the morning he left London for good. Let him go. His train rumbled deep in my mind, and I slept and reawakened over and over. Over and over with the night's recriminations, the abrupt end, the jagged dawn. Then came that plea beneath my window, to which I could not respond. When finally I prised open my eyes, it was afternoon and the blankets were warmed by autumn sun beaming through that very same leaded window.

He was gone. I got on my knees to look out: Saturday strollers in a filigree of spiralling yellow leaves falling from bare limbs.

Who has not exulted in relief? Who doesn't long most for just that, doesn't awaken from some unspeakable crime and check their fingers for blood, actually touch them to their tongue? They're clean! You're safe! You've washed up on the shallows of your manageable waking person and can hunker down in a splash of sunshine, trying to forget the storm that dropped you here.

'What do I want from this life?' I asked myself while poaching two eggs that afternoon. 'From this marshland of dread?' 'I don't want children,' I easily declared. How about becoming an academic? I had been considering applying to do a Master's. I scooped the eggs out of the pan, let them drain and plopped them onto toast. 'Too competitive, and I can't teach.' I salted my lunch. 'I certainly must avoid poetry.' Mopping up a congealing puddle of yolk, I suddenly understood: 'All that I want [and this is all that I've ever wanted, no matter what Sinclair says] is comfort and security, a nine-to-five job in a modestly intellectual environment.' I dropped my plate into the sink with a clatter. 'So I shall become a librarian.'

Then why had I allowed Sinclair to stay with us, to come to Toronto at all? Did I wish to alienate Marjory in the autumn of our pleasant consort? I admit, I had sometimes wondered if my relief might not be complete were she to leave me, blame free, to live out the rest of my life alone. Naturally, I could never leave her.

But Marjory is incredible. My mother lived with us for the last two years of her life and Marjory thrived under her command. She took leave from her secretarial position, her complexion perceptibly brightened, and our meat was more liberally seasoned than my mother advised it should be. Of course, Marjory would complain at the end of each day, but the scowls that attended these diatribes seemed to suggest the sadomasochist's secret smile. Meanwhile, I, for the first and only time in my life, was working a bit of overtime. This was in the early seventies, when Robarts Library had just opened, and the Cataloguing Department – the ladies and I – moved down from Bedford Road into that brand-new concrete book castle. There was tons of work for anyone willing to do it, and with the excuse of Mother's drug costs, I even worked weekends.

Alas, Marjory did not thrive under Sinclair. The first night he was with us she cooked a honeyed ham, with overwintered squash from our garden and Yukon Gold potatoes. I also got busy, clearing the dining-room table of bills and mail, polishing its dulled surface, rifling through boxes in the basement in search of silver candlesticks, polishing those, dashing out for candles, et cetera. I should have taken the clanging and bangs that were shaking the kitchen more seriously, the angry sighs she kept hurling down the stairs at me. Then there was the sphincter-like contraction of her lips. But at seven on the dot she had us all take a side at the candlelit table, our shadows dancing on the wainscotting, and – most embarrassingly – asked me to say grace.

'For what we are about to receive …' I muttered into my shirt collar.

'Amen!' Sinclair loudly declared.

I regarded the silver dome on the platter before me – Marjory's doing. That both of us had felt compelled to outdo the other in an effort at domestic refinement was, ironically, driven by the same desire to establish lines of defence. Cautiously, like a man opening a parcel from his enemy, I lifted the cover and discharged a plume of meaty steam. Marjory, opposite me, was braced to serve squash and potatoes. But Sinclair, to my right, looked to be a bit far from the table, so I got up and adjusted his seat.

'Thank you, Te'di:.'

'Why do you call him that?'

'Eh?'

Her voice was edgy, like a blade that cut her whenever she tried to use it. 'My husband, Ted. Why do you pronounce his name so strangely?'

'Te´di:, you mean?' He laughed.

'It's just that I've never heard anyone call him that. Only "Theodore" or "Ted." Not even normal "Teddy." Your mother didn't call you "Teddy," did she?'

'I'm sorry?'

'I'm trying to remember, did your parents call you "Teddy"? I don't think so.'

'Not that I can recall.' I passed her a plate of ham, which she loaded in concentrated silence as I kept carving.

'To my ear,' mused Sinclair, 'which I have been told is unusually sensitive, "Ted" doesn't sound at all right. Even "Theodore" is better than that, although it's pretty clunky. Maybe if he was a carpenter ...' He smirked in my direction. 'No, never could I have brought myself to call him such a ridiculous, undignified vulgarism as "Ted."'

The plate was fully loaded, but Marjory kept it in front of her and the serving spoon in her hand. Wearing that horrible, false smile, she said, 'Everyone I've ever met has called him "Ted." That's how he introduces himself. His mother called him "Ted" – your mother *always* called you "Ted," I remember now. But what you're saying to me is that what he likes to be called, is called and has always been called is ridiculous and undignified. Have I got that right?'

Sinclair raised and steadied his head, to fix her with a sardonic gaze. 'You got it, Margarine, you're spot on.'

Her face went dead.

'Sinclair! Marjory! My name doesn't matter.'

'I'm sorry, what did you call me?'

'Eh?'

'Did you hear what he called me, Ted?'

'Marjory. He called you Marjory. Sinclair, isn't that what you said?'

'Right, what Te´di: said.'

She dropped the spoon with a crash, placed her serviette on the table and stood. 'Enjoy the dinner, both of you.'

I didn't dare know what to do, so I kept at the meat, racking my mind. I heard her rustling in the hallway closet. The front door opened and slammed.

'Te´di:!' Sinclair grabbed my carving hand. I had reduced a portion of ham to pulp spilling onto the table.

Needless to say, Sinclair did not leave after a couple days, a few days or even a week. Relatively immobile, he mostly stayed in bed, where I'd take him breakfast and lunch. But Marjory insisted, in spite of herself (or to spite me), that we all have dinner together every damn night, which was strained. More-over, she and I were sharing a bed for the first time in years, which in itself would have kept us awake listening to the plinks of each other's blinking through the darkest hours; but Marjory also performed histrionic tosses, while I lay frozen on my back as in the bottom of a lifeboat about to capsize in a storm.

In the middle of the third night, after a day of acid silence and ham salad for supper, Marjory again said, 'Why is he staying with us? What happened to his conference? You will get rid of him, won't you, Ted?'

I assured her I would. 'He's just an old friend, that's all.' I conceded that we'd parted on bad terms.

Two days later Marjory waylaid me just as I emerged out the side of the garage with a handled tray that seemed perfect for serving Sinclair elevenses.

'What's he got on you?' She'd been fertilizing the swollen stalks of roses behind the building.

Setting the tray down, I approached. 'I beg your pardon?'

'What's going on here?'

Again, I asked what she meant, and leaned against the wall. The recent few days had been the warmest we'd had, and all over the place unopened flowers – tulips poking out from freshly raked beds, scilla strewn throughout the lawn, apple and pear buds – were pinking and bluing and yellowing, deepening the colours they were soon to expose.

'I don't understand what's happening. You're acting jittery and neurotic, like when your mother was here and you were always up in the middle of the night, warming milk or checking to make sure that she was still breathing. It's like you're terrified of him, or else you're –'

'Or nothing! I feel sorry for him. What's wrong with that? We were friends and now he's alone. What's he going to do if we throw him out?'

She took a fierce step toward me. 'This is five days already. You said he'd be gone in three. I don't like him and don't want him in my home any longer. Tell me when. I want a date.'

'At the outside, a week.'

'What! From today?'

'No, no, in total.' I retreated back into the garage and concealed the tray under an old bedsheet.

The semicolon has three main uses in present-day English. First, it divides independent clauses in a compound sentence, *without a conjunction*; this is my preferred usage. It implies logical connections yet keeps the statements cleanly separated. The semicolon is used with conjunctions in longer, internally punctuated compound sentences or in complex sentences

(sentences with one or more subordinate clauses); but in both cases the conjunction succeeding the semicolon should coordinate ('and,' 'or,' 'but,' etc.), *not subordinate* ('if,' 'since,' 'when,' because,' etc.). Finally, the semicolon is handy for making tidy lists, when several subordinate clauses depend on the same main verb; when phrases are lengthy, digressive and/or broken up with other marks; and when listed items must emphatically stand alone.

Logic and clarity of expression should be the chief considerations in implementing the semicolon. 'I knew he'd be back; and he was.' This, according to McDermott[12], is correct usage, but I beg to differ. Either omit the conjunction or take advantage of a full stop to start a new sentence, sir. Misusage is a downward spiral of misunderstanding that must be reversed if we are to sustain a well-defined sense of the language, of communication.

On the other hand, it's amazing what you can do without. The *punctus percontativus*, a reversed but not inverted question mark employed in the sixteenth and seventeenth centuries to indicate rhetorical questions, is now long gone.[13] How hard is it today to recognize a question not requiring any answer?

But Sinclair was incorrigible. Yes, I had warmed to his attention, to his affection. He had believed in me and I'd badly needed that. Then he took me to bed, when I'd drunk too much brandy and my legs wouldn't get me back to campus. At least Marjory respected boundaries. We made love. Marjory and I made love. Released, I finally could rest, on my side of the bed, listening to clapping chestnut leaves in summer, or cold reminders tapping on the glass during my favourite season, winter. I didn't cherish Sinclair's memory; just the opposite, I detest it even today. Only his absence has ever been of any

12 McDermott, 51.
13 Parkes, 53.

value to me. I did not want to see him again, I never wanted to see him again, his presence in my life has been absolutely debilitating.

That first week he was with us I'd sit on the foot of his bed, with the door ajar, and we'd chat in low voices.

'Did you sleep well?'

'No, my chest hurts.'

'Your chest? I'd better get you to a doctor.'

'No, Te´di:, no.' He burbled a laugh. 'Yes, it's still you. Off to the doctor, wringing your hands.'

I smiled.

'See, I pushed you and pushed you. Then I left you alone and you were lost.'

'What do you mean?'

'I mean you never wanted to live, mister. Now you probably don't want to die. You want the womb. Am I the only one who's tried to tug you out?'

'What?'

'Has any other man sucked your cock?'

Blushing, I stared out the window and didn't answer.

'Yeah, well, I haven't changed either, and I don't need medicine for my heart. I want the last beat to be mine, all mine.' His eyes floated about vaguely, seemed to focus on my knee, and he continued: 'The stroke that's going to clear up this zero-sum calculation is the sum of my life.' He suddenly glared at me. 'That's the way to understand it.'

I squirmed. His eyes were wet. Mine shot back to the window. Soon I patted his blanketed foot and left.

'Listen, Sinclair,' I said at the end of the first week. 'Marjory's pretty upset. Didn't you say you were coming for a few days? It's already been a week.'

'This isn't Marjory's business. Tell her I'll be dead in six months.'

'Dead?' I looked at him. 'Come on, that's not fair. This is her house too. At least you could be more gracious.'

Sinclair sat up, flushed. 'More gracious? Put yourself in my shoes. Look what she's done.' He signalled at me with a limp hand.

'To me?'

He slumped back. 'Never mind. Just tell her I'll be gone in six months.' He closed his eyes.

He had made an effort, in his way. He hadn't called her 'Margarine' since the blow-up of day one, and he liked to holler, 'Morning, Marjory!' from his bed when she hurried past. Now, half an hour after I asked him to try harder, he waved her into the room and extolled the eggs I'd poached for him, sprinkling his praise with small suggestions for the perfection of her technique, such as garnishing with fresh dill. But it was too little, too late: the deadline was written all over us all. I'll transcribe verbatim my decisive communication with Marjory, once again in the garden.

She was on all fours with rubbered knees, gouging the vegetable bed with one of those triple-clawed, stubby-handled hoes. The grass was ready for a first cut, so I said, 'I see the lawn needs mowing,' to prompt her.

She sat up on her heels, removed her gloves and, like a large grey squirrel, repeatedly swept her hands across her face and over her head, taming some errant hairs, before, in profile, she replied, 'Yes, it does,' and stroked the green shoots.

'Maybe I'll do it tomorrow.'

'If you like.'

'Do you want me to do it this afternoon?'

'It doesn't matter.'

'Oh-kay.'

'I've decided to stay with my sister.'

'But she lives in Parry Sound.'

'And?'

'Surely that's not necessary, Marjory. We needn't be disturbed by this.'

'But we are.' A robin was stalking the lawn for worms. We both paused to watch it yank a wriggler to light and hop off with it hanging from its beak.

'How long will you be gone?'

'Until he's gone. I will not come back until he's gone.'

I nodded. I nodded and gave my hands a final, especially thorough wring in absolute sincerity. 'When do you want me to take you?'

'In an hour.' She tossed her gloves into the wheelbarrow on top of a bag of composted manure and envelopes of seeds.

Driving north from Toronto in early May is gloomily regressive. I've said my favourite season's winter, but winter that directly succeeds an aborted spring – such being the impression one gets driving north – I find sick and disheartening. It's like watching a film played in reverse without having seen it forward in the first place; or worse, seeing it in reverse immediately after having watched it properly, so that the jerky backward movement is all burlesque repetition and disillusionment. Hazy green clouds in the branches of urban maples quickly disappear, leaving the poplar's dangly brown florescence, eventually nullified as well. Nature must be starving, or dead. Lawns are coffee-coloured, caked in rotting leaves. Suddenly there's snow again! Dirty little fingers of it pointing out from every black fencerow or hidden in crevasses of the Canadian Shield.

I didn't get out of the car at Marjory's sister's. They have a long driveway crowded by pines and scrubby oaks, and at five o'clock, when I dropped her off, it was deep in shadow. What could I have said anyhow? What possible explanation could there be for this abrupt departure so late in the day? I popped the trunk and killed the engine to say goodbye. 'I'm sorry' is what I wanted to say.

'You should be,' she'd have replied.

'I don't know what's happening, Marjory. Can you forgive me?'

'But you're hurting me.'

'Come back with me. Try to put up with him. Maybe he'll be dead by the time we get home, if we drive slowly, if we stop for supper.'

'You've betrayed me.'

'Nonsense. I haven't betrayed you.'

'You're betraying me.'

She might not have said those things. Maybe she would have come back if I'd begged her. I find it hard to believe, though. Sinclair was a thorn piercing both of our hearts. Until he died, it was better to suffer alone. 'I'll call you, Marjory.'

'Okay.'

'I'm sorry.'

'Okay.'

'I love you.'

'Okay.'

There's no simple darkness, is there? My headlights cut shaky paths down the two-lane highway, through the forest, and when two became four we were many and it was night. With jewelled tails we raced into the city, into light, where Sinclair awaited my return.

I was puzzled to see our house unlighted as I parked in the driveway. Even Sinclair's bedroom, why was its side window black? I thought, 'Sinclair!' and crashed out of the car. I was up the front steps, fumbling with my keys, and threw open the door. 'Sinclair! Sinclair!' I slapped on the lights. 'Sinclair.' Up the stairs. 'Sinclair!' Bedroom empty. 'Sinclair?'

'In here.' His voice seemed to sound from the far end of a pipe, or the bottom of a well. 'I'm in the bathroom.'

I burst in – it was pitch-black – and hit the switch: there, in the dry tub, shivered my miserable, naked friend.

'When do you think you might put fucking handles in here?'

'Gosh, I …'

'I've been stuck like this for hours.'

'Sinclair! …'

'Are you coming to help me out, or what?'

Was I going to help him out? Well, yes, certainly I hadn't any choice. But my mind raced around its exhausted track in pursuit of some miraculously hands-off way to right him as I cringed closer to his ever larger and more glaring nakedness.

'What's the matter with you, Teddy?' Not Te′di:. An ominous shift. I'd forgotten how he'd pronounced my name so bracingly straight whenever we were close, his tongue touching the dental consonant with a tenderness reminiscent of young love and those shameless namesake necklaces that the smitten fondle, one letter at a time. I clomped across the bathroom in my sturdy outdoor shoes, with a burgundy towel held at arm's length, like a doomed bullfighter, like a bathhouse slave.

'What are you doing? I need a hand, not a towel.'

I draped it over the shower-curtain rod. There he lay, a crumpled heap of hirsute flesh. His privates – the penis – which my eyes wouldn't ignore, looked obscenely small beneath a substantial fold of belly, while its vermicular mouth, its ophidian eye – that dreadful little orifice – peered blindly out of the hoary bush, like an unforgettably sinister suggestion. I extended my two stony arms and left it up to him to figure out what to do with them.

'Come on, mister, give me a hand. You want me to monkey my own way out of here? Get down here and give me a hand.'

I held my breath and looped my right arm under his clammy, furry left armpit. He partially supported himself on the edge of the tub with his right hand, and then flung it over my shoulder so that we were caught in a staggering embrace.

One page being rubbed against the next: that's the noise our parched old skins made, chafing, until I had him tightly wrapped in a towel and propped against his walker, at which point I collapsed onto the toilet seat and hid my face in my hands. Sinclair muttered, 'Nothing's changed,' and stamped away to the guest room to get dressed for what turned out to be a very pleasant Chinese-food dinner.

Sinclair was to live until December, approximately seven more months, and this period of cohabitation can be conveniently broken into three phases, the first beginning with the bathtub extrication and ending in September like the summer. During this time Sinclair didn't leave the house, and, but for the procurement of necessities, I didn't go further than the back garden. I admit I didn't discourage his seclusion. Perhaps I even encouraged it, although I would not say I enforced it. My next-door neighbour Tahir was partly to blame, with his baneful eye and prickly moustache. He'd lean over the fence and ask after Marjory, to whom he'd promised a pail of his Bokashi liquid nutrient concoction for her vegetables. I'd mutter something about her sister, or else I'd enunciate perfectly clearly, 'She's visiting her sister,' looking him straight in the eye. He'd nod dubiously and run his gaze over the weed-choked vegetable plot where a cucumber was likely nudging itself onto the lawn.

I called Marjory just once, finding her sister's icy 'One minute' a bit too much to bear. But I did receive Marjory's calls, with increasing infrequency, until some time in the middle of June when we wordlessly agreed that there was nothing to discuss so long as Sinclair was extant. In compensation, I periodically fiddled with her flowers (if Tahir was not around) – strapped on her rubber knees and sprinkled water over the drooping foxgloves up against the back of the house, yanking out several of the largest weeds. It was a feeble effort, especially considering that my semi-colon project was boxed and on hold and morning after morning I reawakened to another brimming dayful of time.

'That damned garden got the better of me,' I told Sinclair at the end of August, pointing out his window at the sere lawn.

Often we'd sit there in silence, enjoying the vista of brown or russet shingled roofs and of the willowtop swaying against the sky. Sometimes we'd tell each other stories from our lives. It turned out he hadn't written a poem in forty-odd years, a stunning revelation for me, who still saw him as poetry incarnate. He said he'd called it renunciation at the time, but in truth he had lost heart. 'Too much work for nothing,' he declared. I wanted to know precisely where, when and how his muse had left him, but my unintended zeal seemed to stop him from elaborating. He regarded me askance, with a bemused expression playing on his lips, and moved on, on to adventures in Morocco and Algeria. Eventually he'd migrated north to Dalmatia, where each August, for years, he'd joined a pair of Balkan lovers in their hideaway in the Velebit Mountains, descending into Zadar at night for dips in the Adriatic and for wine and black risotto in the Roman Quarter. 'Wait till I tell you about Mozambique, Teddy.'

My small life embarrassed me. I confessed it, the relief I felt in the windowless stacks, or plunking new cards into catalogues in those leisurely days before computers. I explained my love-hate relationship with the Collection Development Department, where I began my career, in the grand old Sigmund Samuel Library at the University of Toronto, dreaming of freedom in the search for out-of-print titles. But suddenly I'd be shaken, literally, by an irate professor who had seized both my arms and was demanding to know why we still didn't have a single copy of his book, *What's the Matter? Dialectical Materialism Redressed*, one of a zillion textbooks I was supposed to have acquired while the more aggressive members of the department were jetting off to New York for an auction or to Dallas to assess an estate. My reflexively contrite response to this tyrant earned me a second chance to order his essential work; but before I could phone the distributor, word of the assault had spread to the cataloguers – a dry troop of bespectacled women with large or narrow tweed-skirted rears and thick ankles who marched to and from the cafeteria thrice daily to exchange their husbands' opinions on Communism or the Red Ensign. They wasted no time in extending an invitation for me to join them for tea that afternoon, where they demanded to know exactly what had happened, and – breaking scones – then vied to outdo one another with similar stories of abuse suffered at the hands of our august professors.

I laughed so hard I wept, remarkable for a man who rarely laughs if anyone's watching. Obstinately practical, mulishly content to complain, in complete mastery of their muted bodies, these women were ideal, the perfect dusky flock to shelter me until I was ready to retire from the stormy world of academia. By the end of the month I'd switched departments, with the blessing of the Head Librarian.

In the early days of Robarts there were hundreds of cataloguers, slaving from nine to five, unable to keep pace with the unprecedented rate of acquisition. On principle, we refused to get excited, and would never miss a groan when we installed ourselves at a typewriter to cut into a package of virgin catalogue cards. Then at lunch we'd go in cliques to compare notes on our co-workers and grumble about the sub-par weather.

But the department had been gutted by the time I left. Scarcely two dozen of us remained, and still we suffered accusations of redundancy. A techie invasion had been headed by a new Head Librarian in the late eighties (coincidentally, about the time zebra mussels appeared so insidiously in Lake Ontario) and soon we were surrounded, like gentle, plant-eating mammals, without any effective defences against these virtually illiterate dogs of progress. Many of us quickly succumbed to retirement, others were shot, but seven or eight of us clung to some special bit of knowledge we were convinced we possessed and took humiliating retraining courses, only to suffer our juvenile superiors' exasperated sighs and nauseating cologne. We called ourselves the 'tackies' – my coinage, derivative of 'tactile' (Sinclair spluttered a laugh) – and we were wont to linger over make-work projects in shadowy corners, biting our tongues and waiting, minds stuffed with nice stiff cards, for the techies to trip up.

'Outside of that,' I concluded, 'Marjory and I went to Florida once and disliked it. To Nova Scotia once.' I puzzled. 'I guess my life's been filled with such modest pleasures, I can't quite recall them.'

His eyes accused me, but warmly, twinkling in their bed of wrinkles.

Thus we passed the summer pleasantly, the best way I could have imagined, in separate beds; except for his twice-weekly baths, I was comfortable with our relationship and true to Marjory. Until one fateful day in mid-September – a Sunday – when I, on a whim, suggested we drive down to the lakefront for a walk.

We were enjoying an Indian summer. The long shoreline park whizzed with roller skaters and runners, and cracked with laughing children, while lovers and picnicking families dotted the grass. Sinclair moved deliberately, if slowly, trailblazing with his walker the asphalt path that wound around defoliating ash trees, our ponderous, bent bodies frustrating the quick, oncoming, sideswiping, rear-ending youths who congested around us and squeezed past, one at a time. Driven inward by the adjacent expressway traffic and the smog-scattered sunlight, we kept our eyes to the ground, squinting against gritty cyclones of dry leaves and trash. A bench stood vacant some twenty feet back from the water, under the trees, and I took Sinclair's arm to direct him there.

'Hmm, that's better.' He settled back and released his walker, which I moved beside him before I sat down and made to draw an especially spirited breath that was interrupted when a faint whiff of sewage needled my nostrils and induced a fit of sneezing.

When my eyes cleared, I beheld the lake, slick and placid, mirroring a milky sky. I could distinguish no horizon in the grey offing, but a dozen or so distant tiny sails caught my drifting eye, seemed to point to something mythic, an impending invasion, a good old-fashioned sacking of the city after which nothing would ever be the same. I nudged Sinclair to show him.

'Huh?'

'Look at that.'

'At what?'

'The boats.'

'The boats. Jesus, Teddy. A bunch of silly sailboats. You sound like a rocking-chair biddy.'

'No, I wasn't … Not because they're pretty. They're haunting, don't you think they look haunting?'

With a grunt, he struck his walker to the ground. 'Take me home. I don't want to talk to you anymore.'

'Sinclair!'

'What is this?' He twirled his hand above his head. 'I'm dying and here we are living like a couple of old maids, whiling away the days, mooning about the past and remarking on the fucking weather.'

'I though we were having a very –'

'You thought, you thought. Maybe you should try on your own soul for size. You suck the life out of me! I shrink every day that you're near. So sweep me up and drop me in the dustbin when you're done, okay?'

'Honestly, Sinclair, I don't know what you're –'

'No, you wouldn't, would you, you dishonest little cock-sucker? This is precisely where we left off. Closeted old queer. Fine, you win.' He reached for the foot of his overturned walker, tried to grab it, but toppled off the bench and in lurches slowly, wilfully rolled until he came to a stop, supine with a vacant smile, beside a fringe of long brown grass by the caged-stone retaining wall. 'No more, old Ted! I'm done.' He lifted his head and saw me glaring, with my head cocked, standing between him and the bench. 'What's the matter, Ted, I've ruffled your feathers? No, you know what you are?'

Tonguing my molars, I didn't reply.

'You're nothing but a sigh.' He propped himself up. 'If I have to listen to another detail of that hateful, bleak life you've led, I'll probably take my own. Maybe that's what I ought to do, hey? And take you with me. Wouldn't that be romantic? What have *you* got to lose?'

On that train of rhetorical questions our lately reactivated relationship entered its second, markedly spiteful phase, two months during which time Sinclair took interminable daily stamps (or stands, from what I could gather watching from afar, for every ten steps he would stop to catch his breath) about the neighbourhood and I went back to work on my punctuation project, studying copies of fifteenth-century manuscripts to better understand early usage of the *virgula suspensiva*, which evolved into the comma. Until this helpful mark entered the general repertory of punctuation in the fourteenth century, the writer and the scribe could indicate only *major* medial pauses, using the *punctus elevatus* (which became the colon), employed when 'the sense was complete but the sentence was not'[14] (a role eventually assumed by the semicolon). With the advent of the *virgula*, pointing *minor* medial pauses became possible as well, especially useful where neither the sense *nor* the sentence was complete. I took Sinclair directly home, rolled out our couch in the living room and transferred him down there so that he could function more or less independently. The next morning I angrily cut him a key.

But I couldn't take my office back. It stank of Sinclair. I closed the door and went to Robarts every morning, leaving his breakfast on the radiator by the front door and putting him out of my mind until I had to return home in the evening to feed him. Only his damned baths, which I performed with exaggerated disgust, interfered with this satisfactory new routine.

I told myself I was the one with the level head, as I took umbrage behind another stack of books at my regular carrel. On our way home from the lake I'd shouted at him, with both hands on the steering wheel. When a man who never shouts shouts, look out. 'Do you think I enjoy taking care of you?' 'I should evict you.' Worse, 'Feel free to do yourself in – only leave me out of it.' Predictable stuff, but I think it unnerved him, which felt good, to cut him at last.

'Bathtime, Sinclair,' I'd say in an acid tone. Saturdays and Wednesdays, at six in the evening. By early November, only Saturdays.

'Screw off. I can do it myself.' He was sitting on the edge of the rollout couch in his bathrobe.

---

14 Parkes, 42.

'Now, take my arm.'

We lurched up the stairs.

'Don't look at me.'

'I'd rather eat shit.'

He pulled off his robe and I complained about the stink.

'When are you going to put a handlebar beside the toilet?'

'Use your walker to stand up.'

'It's downstairs.'

'You hardly use this bathroom.'

'What about the one downstairs?'

'Use your damn walker. Now get in, the water's hot.' I wrestled him into the tub, sweating and gnashing my teeth.

My sleeps were torturous those two months. I'd plunge into precisely imagined nightmares, like the one where I get up from bed to go to the bathroom and find Sinclair soaking in a tub of densely steaming water. I go to grab him, to pull him out, but he starts thrashing and water's splashing over the side with great slaps onto the tiles until we both crash down on one of these waves and he's panting on top of me. Mid-scream, I awaken, or so I imagine, but in fact enter upon a series of punctuational transformations involving harmonization according to an abstruse, consciously incomprehensible principle of balance in pause and implication that I'm trying to arrange with Post-it notes. I wake up needing to pee, and suffering a painful erection; but, fixating on how he'd hear my footsteps in the living room directly below me, I lie in a knot for a long time first.

One evening in early November – once again, a Sunday – I stopped for fish and chips at a pub on Broadview where I've eaten off and on for the past few years and am acquainted with some of the regulars. I had been feeling decreasingly concerned with Sinclair and would often leave his supper – a bowl of brown beans, for instance – in the microwave before I went to the library in the morning. Or I'd drop a doggy bag by his door upon returning. I'd done the former on this particular day. The waitress brought me my fish at the bar, and I was just opening a packet of tartar sauce when someone behind me shouted, 'There he is!' To my right and left, men hopped off their stools, while the owner, Jimmy (who mistakenly calls me 'Tim'), pulled out a clipboard and stopwatch from under the bar and yelled, 'Ready, guys?'

'Okay, Jimmy …' They were clustered at the picture window facing the street. 'Three, two, one, go!'

Beep, Jimmy started the watch, and then hurried over to join them. I was curious, naturally. Although my supper was cooling, I left it and approached the tangle of men.

'What's going on?' I asked Roger, a former schoolteacher, famous at the restaurant for his skill with crossword puzzles.

'One sec, one sec.'

I nudged in to get a look.

It was nearly dark outside, so I had to strain to see past our reflections in the glass. There seemed nothing remarkable … until I noticed Sinclair, crossing over to the east side of Broadview, stamping his way along in the streetlit gloaming. 'What are you fellows looking at?'

'That old guy, over there. Look at him go.'

'Him?' He was approaching the far curb.

They started chanting, 'Go, go, go!' Sinclair hefted his walker onto the sidewalk, stepped up, and the men cheered.

'Two minutes, thirty-seven,' said Jimmy.

They were timing him crossing the street.

As I wolfed down my tepid meal, I got the dirt from Jimmy. The week before, Sinclair – nobody knew I had any connection with him and they called him 'Toad' – had made a scene. He'd come in for coffee, taking a seat at the bar and setting his walker behind him. After slurping down a few cupfuls, he threw insufficient change on the counter, spun around and toppled onto the floor where he was expecting to find the walker, which Roger had moved out of the way. Sinclair went ballistic. He called Roger, who was apologetically helping him to his feet, a 'gushing girlie,' threatened to sue Jimmy for 'everything but his balls,' collected the coins he'd underpaid with and left. Hence this game of revenge, the 'Toadpool.'

Here's how it worked: a daily two-dollar wager could be placed on Sinclair's street-crossing time (apparently he appeared on that northwest corner, travelling east toward home, every day), but that was only for a lark, according to Jimmy, who recorded everybody's bets and awarded the pot to whoever came closest. The real excitement was in the 'Toad Cross Calendar.' He brought it over, a regular calendar with a name written under each date. 'I'll be taking bets for January soon.' These were ten-dollar wagers, put on the anticipated date when Sinclair would finally fail to cross the street before the light turned red. 'You want in?'

'I sure do.'

'There's a few open dates.' He scanned the calendar. 'The 14th and 16th of November, and December 27th.'

'I want all three.'

'Atta boy, Tim. Now we'll get January going.'

I handed him the thirty dollars.

I did not return to the restaurant until the 14th of November, a week and a half later, but in my pocket calendar and in my mind I crossed off the passing days, each a potential stumbling block to the pair I'd marked with S's. S for success, S for sink and savour, for sadism. I stuck to my serious study of the semi-colon, and if Sinclair said something galling, say he sneered at me in my sleep or scorned me with his sex as I stuffed him into the bathtub, I simply smiled. My superstitious side stopped me from even seeking to know whether he'd kept succeeding at crossing.

Why did I do all this? Don't ask. The whys get you in trouble – they make fiction of your life. This is what I did. On the 14th I rose early and took a methodical bath. I shaved the 'beard' that had been collecting like gossamer on my cheeks since my fight with Sinclair. I clipped my fingernails, flossed my teeth and energetically polished my brown oxfords. Then I slipped into a beige-striped button-down shirt and a pair of grey slacks, cleaned and pressed, and I buttoned up a maroon mohair cardigan. My neck was too exposed, I decided, combing my hair in the mirror, and unearthed a burgundy cravat.

The analogy of the duel would be unsatisfactory here. We'd best drop deeper into history, to when monsters were still real. Let me liken myself to Beowulf, addressing a final boast to his men on the wind-beaten brow that overlooked Grendel's lair. With what gravity he must have prepared himself on that grim Nordic morn! I was stamping my feet outside the restaurant when Jimmy unlocked the door at 8 a.m. 'Is he still in the running?'

'Your big day, eh, Tim?'

Little did he know.

Roger soon joined me at the table by the window. I don't know him very well, but my confidence was riding high, so, slicing a sausage in two, I said, 'Mark my words, the game is up.'

He didn't look up from his crossword. 'That's what Dan said yesterday.'

'This is different,' I said into my scrambled eggs. This was something entirely different.

Sinclair has always been cunning. I've even suspected he's telepathic. I tried to keep focused on the street, but he knew what he was doing and postponed our reckoning for as long as possible. It was late afternoon when his bent figure finally appeared and I shouted, 'There he is! There's that stupid toad.'

Everyone crowded around.

He stopped on the corner despite a green light. 'What's he doing?'

'Waiting for the light to change to red so he'll have a full green to cross on.'

'That son of a bitch.'

'Don't worry, he's on his last legs. He almost didn't make it yesterday.'

I smiled gratefully.

'Okay, Jimbo, you ready?' said Roger. 'Here we go. Three, two, one …'

Sinclair lifted his walker, set it down on the street and, after stepping off the sidewalk, proceeded with slow, deliberate movements. He was like a mule, or a conquistador, everything depended on his successful passage. Could everyone see that? Could they see those strained tendons shaping his bent black coat, the hard-wired will I was determined to snap? He was just past mid-street when the red hand began flashing. Someone rhythmically patted the table. Sinclair inched onward, past the second set of streetcar tracks. Stop, I implored – pulsing hand, go still. One broken line, one lane: all that was left for him to cross. In five excruciating steps he'd half done it, and everything – my hope, my flushed complexion, the uncharacteristic enthusiasm that had seized me – it all drained away. A few more heaves and grunts and it was over.

I slammed the table with both hands. Nobody said anything. He would have to be weakened before the 16th, scarcely a day away.

On the 15th I escaped the house early, having hardly slept a wink. I left Sinclair his usual breakfast on the radiator, but with light white bread for toast, a thin spread of margarine and diet jam. In my carrel I was meditating on the etymological and actual relationship between 'punctilio,' 'punctilious' and 'punctuation,' when it struck me anew how deeply moral – even moralistic – is the tone pervading most works on punctuation. G. V. Carey, perhaps the chief punctuational didacticist of the twentieth century, responds to a series of fragments treated as separate sentences as follows: 'What is the point of this sort of thing? Is it meant to convey a subtle form of humour or merely to be snappy? I can see nothing but wilful murder of the mother tongue, scarcely more excusable than any other form of matricide.'[15] Suddenly, starving Sinclair seemed inexcusable. If I wasn't going to give him supper, I'd better make a mid-afternoon meal instead.

I rushed home. Microwaved a drastically calorie-reduced fettucini alfredo. Left again. But couldn't concentrate on my project anymore, so I went to a disappointing matinee.

Come dawn of the 16th I was ruthless. There was too much at stake. I left him no breakfast, easing my conscience, as I tumbled out the door before seven o' clock, with plans for a nice juicy steak when the day was finally complete. I had not shaved nor bathed. It was Saturday and Jimmy's would not open until nine.

To my mind that was our first winter morning. The sidewalks were slick with rime, a dark slate sky seemed to drop as it lightened, and I shivered my way through the streets without scarf, hat or gloves, periodically stopping at a doughnut shop to warm up.

'You all right there, Tim?' Jimmy asked when he unlocked the door.

'How do you mean?'

---

15 Carey, 14.

'You look sick.'

'Just tired.'

'Come on in.'

'Well?'

It took him a moment. 'Oh yeah, you've got another shot at the bank today, don't you? Yup, he made it yesterday.'

I took my place by the window and waited irritably for breakfast. The first flurries of the season struck the window with sharp ticks. I eyed an icy patch in the middle of the crossing, but soon a cursèd transit worker descended from his dingdong streetcar to plunge a pail into a box on the corner and strew salt all over the sweet spot.

'What are you grumbling about?'

'Nothing, Roger, nothing.'

You can't predict Sinclair, I can tell you that, Roger. We finished breakfast. Jimmy refilled our cups. Our view of the street was increasingly cross-hatched with snowfall.

'This hardly seems fair,' said Roger.

I shrugged, reminding him that nobody could have predicted when snow would come, nor, for that matter, what infirmities might affect Toad, and I exaggerated the margin with which he had succeeded two days before. Roger opened his mouth but I cut him off. 'There he is! Jimmy!'

This was unprecedented, according to anything I'd heard. It was hardly past ten in the morning. But unmistakably, that was Sinclair's corvine shadow blackening the usual corner. Where the hell was Jimmy? I bellowed, 'Toad Crossing!' There was a crash in the kitchen and he came running.

'Already?' He grabbed his stuff behind the bar. 'Okay, just tell me. Count me down.'

Sinclair was readying himself. He adjusted his scarf, then his grip on the walker, and said something that was just a puff of condensation to us. The snow blew thicker and harder, swirling around him, dry little particles that collected in shifting ribbons until a gust curled a tongue of the stuff up into the air, into the eyes of pedestrians. The four or five men around me started roaring like bison, stamping their feet, and I did the count-down: 'Three, two, one, NOW.'

Sinclair hesitated. All of us felt it, like a static shock. Then he lowered his walker to the street. Roger pounded the table with his fists. 'He's going. All right.'

He took a step.

'Look at him, he's going strong.'

I couldn't seem to focus properly. I wiped my eyes.

'Go, go, go.'

I looked up at Jimmy – who was tonguing the corner of his mouth, with a close eye on the stopwatch – and shivered. Lack of sleep? Bracing my head between my hands, I tried to home in on Sinclair's weakened determination.

Suddenly he stopped, just past halfway. 'What's he doing?' His shoulders shifted from side to side under a thin mantle of snow. He shook his snowy head. 'Oh, Tim, something's up.' Somebody wondered aloud if he was having a stroke. I felt sick. But I was glued to the seat.

Then Roger perspicaciously observed, 'His walker's snagged.'

'Oh, thank god,' I murmured. In a crack or a pothole or the streetcar track.

'Heartless bugger,' someone joked.

An SUV that had been making a left-hand turn, contingent on Sinclair's sustained forward motion, found itself hemmed in by oncoming cars. All blew their horns. Sinclair's shoulders shed some snow. The men around me jammed tighter and tighter, until they squeezed out the inevitable question: 'Shouldn't we help him?'

'Ask Tim.'

'Just a minute.' I stayed focused. Two pedestrians appeared to be separately coming to his aid. Horns kept blaring; the traffic-light timer was steadily counting down; an approaching street-car rang its bell for good measure. Suddenly Sinclair threw up his hands, releasing his walker, and stumbled, a free man, around it and toward the far sidewalk. One of the pedestrians swept in from behind and hooked his left arm, which Sinclair tried momentarily to reappropriate before he latched onto the stranger with his right hand as well and they hobbled together. The red hand kept flashing. The other Samaritan approached the abandoned walker and tugged it free. Jesus, was Sinclair going to make it? He was a few feet from the curb when the hand froze. He had hardly a step to go when the traffic light went yellow. But that huge suv, finally able to complete its turn, eclipsed him just as the light turned red, so next thing we knew he was safely on the sidewalk, proceeding with his helper in the direction of home.

'He didn't make it,' I said.

'Yeah, he did.'

'No.' I had no confidence. 'Where's Jimmy? Jimmy, he didn't make it, did he?'

'Sorry, Tim, I couldn't tell. See, the timer's still running.'

'Didn't anyone see that? He definitely didn't make it.' Everyone muttered non-committally, except the one man, who again demurred. I snatched my jacket, pushed through them and left.

Have I a hard heart? It's a question I've put to myself before. Have a heart, have a heart. I gave heartfelt thanks to the crema-tor who transferred Sinclair's ashes from the puzzling black cube into his urn for me. 'What happens to the metal in their teeth?' I asked him. 'Or if they have a plate in their head or pins in their bones?' He was evasive, but the answer didn't matter. Sinclair had no gold teeth.

No, really, I don't mean to be like that. It's just that I get confused going on like this, all these months in this empty house have made me feel quite unknown. Not like Te´di: or Ted or Teddy. Maybe something like the Theodore of boyhood.

I *will* call Marjory, perhaps, tomorrow. (*Nota bene*: I've here employed Lord Edward John Moreton Drax Plunket Dunsany's punctuational *bête noire*, the ambiguously comma'd enclosure of 'perhaps.'[16] Which is in doubt, the phone call itself or the anticipated time?) She's been leaving messages since the first March thaw. Clips and barbs. Snarls coiled around her helplessness. But I've frozen. I sit on a stool beside the phone and periodically pick up the receiver. The dial drone continues as long as I pay the bill. Listen long enough – not that long, actually – and something somewhere begins ringing, but I put the receiver quickly down to avoid an operator's scolding. On the other hand, sometimes chastisement – especially anonymous chastisement – is just what the doctor ordered. How disappointing it was when, after I'd waited white-knuckled to see what that ring would deliver, all she could say, over and over again, was 'Please hang up and try your call again. Please hang up. This is a recording.' I ought to call Marjory. I've got to call Marjory. For god's sake, all her things are still here.

On the other hand, I won't. The only thing certain is that I'll toil at my desk in the guest room with its narrow view of the garden, where the apple trees are again at odds with each other, an on-year for one, all a-blush and a-tremble, a disappointing off- for the other. It's already May, but sometimes I still smell Sinclair in here.

---

16 Edward John Moreton Drax Plunket Dunsany, Baron, Litt.D., FRSL, 'Among the Ruins,' *Essays by Divers Hands, Being the Transactions of the Royal Society of Literature of the U.K.*, Vol. XXI. Ed. Walter De La Mare (London: Oxford University Press/Humphrey Milford, 1944), 21.

In April I was devastated by an essay on punctuation by a homosexual academic whose self-confessed preoccupations are opera, sex and Freud.[17] That he should venture into the arcane world of pointing and that I took his opinions to heart defies reason. He says, 'Semicolons are pretentious and overactive.' Worse, 'They [semicolons] place two clauses in some kind of relation to one another [sic] but relieve the writer of saying exactly what the relation is.' Finally, 'The semicolon has become so hateful to me that I feel almost morally compromised when I use it.'

I literally broke down in tears at the end of this essay, so at odds with my own beliefs. Since then I've been rebuilding myself from the full stop up.

The period. The *punctus*. The progenitor of them all. 'The period comes at the end of a sentence, strictly of a periodic sentence, but now loosely apprehended as any sentence, even if it consists of only one word [e.g., "No."].'[18] Sense and sentence are complete, as in the elliptical example, which, spelled out, would be, 'No, you are mistaken.' or 'No, I will not.', ad infinitum.

The third and final phase of my relationship with Sinclair began when nobody could say whether he'd made it across the street in time. I stood lost on the sidewalk in an angry blow of snow, but overhead the clouds were breaking up and becoming inlaid with blue. I, also, was full of gaps and ice. Where my heart's supposed to be there were no guarantees. I spotted Sinclair's walker on the far corner. How could that have been left behind? Useless Samaritans. I crossed against the lights and snatched it up as one does one's shameful refuse.

17 Paul Robinson, 'The Philosophy of Punctuation,' *Opera, Sex, and Other Vital Matters* (Chicago: University of Chicago Press, 2002), 305–6.

18 Eric Partridge, *You Have a Point There: A Guide to Punctuation and Its Allies* (London: Routledge, 1953), 9.

I tried to carry the walker in front of me, and then off my hip. Even on my back. But it was too awkward and my exhaustion became such a burden that in the end I actually used it to walk. I remember the house being pitch-dark except for a light in the living-room window. But how can that be? It wasn't even noon and I swear that the sky was blowing clear.

Forgiveness. A second chance. The greatest relief of all. No, let me correct that: the greatest relief – the sharpest remorse – is, once again, oblivion. Not death, I don't mean that. I mean the place where the blood from our dream went. I set Sinclair's walker beside the radiator and knocked on the living-room door.

'Come in.'

He was in bed. His hair was wet. His clothes, heaped on the floor. The room smelt powerfully of man.

'Sinclair, what happened?' I asked, weakened by deceit and aching. 'Your walker was on the lawn. Your clothes are wet. Look at your face. What's the meaning of this?'

He didn't answer any of my questions. Instead he growled, 'Whyn't you leave me breakfast this morning?' His chin trembled.

I say, Sinclair, Sinclair, please forgive me. For god's sake, I'm sorry. I beg you, Sinclair. I literally begged him. You've never left me alone. Even now your urn's on the windowsill, blocking my view, and I often wish a storm would come and blow it over so that I could vacuum up your remains in the morning. The sentence is not finished. No, the sense is not complete. Your walker's beside Marjory's wheelbarrow in the garage, beside her gloves and rubber knees, and sometimes I'll sit there and sigh, behind closed doors. I'm sorry. He knew that from the first.

Before he slipped into a coma he told me he'd never thought my poetry was all that good. By this time I'd moved him upstairs to my bed. I was sleeping downstairs on the couch and doing anything I could to make him comfortable and to punish myself. I slept under an itchy blanket and left the window open. I climbed the stairs five times a night to refresh his hot-water bottle. I helped him on and off the toilet. Bathed him. Ate his leftovers. I said I was going to bury him in my family's plot, but he said, 'Teddy, why do you think I brought that urn when I came to die for you?'

He propped himself up on an elbow and pointed to a pile of books. 'Pass me that one.' He opened it. An envelope was stuck inside the cover. With unsteady fingers he unfolded a very brown piece of paper.

'What is it?'

'"The Closest Man."' He looked at me.

'My poem …'

'Here.'

I reached.

'Burn it with me,' he said, and left my poem in my hand, period.

ઐ

**Greg Denton Dons
Golden Threads
in Anticipation**

His are reminiscent of van Gogh's: thick ump– no, impasto, impressionistic. Heavy brush strokes, a lot like van Gogh. Smitty, I'm serious, he wants to paint my portrait. Here's what he wrote:

Dear Mr. Denton,

As a painter named Greg Denton, I'd like to paint all the Greg Dentons I can locate and hang them together in an exhibition. I would be honoured if you agreed to participate. Please mail me a photograph of yourself. I, in turn, will contact you once the project is complete and a date has been set for the opening. To give you a sense of my work, I've enclosed the invitation from my last show.

Yours truly,
Greg Denton
11 Cobbled Lane
Guelph, ON

Next I showed it to Junior, who pulls taps at the club.

– So you think you're going to do it?

– Why not?

– Didn't you say his style's outdated?

– Junior, I'm not saying I'm convinced about this Greg Denton, but what the heck, I don't mind helping an aspiring artist.

That damn Smitty:

– You probably saw that new movie. Old Pollock the pop hero, the tortured genius. Hah, Greggo will be delivering a lecture on Warhol next week, huh, pal?

I could have been an artist. Who does he think he is?

Junior's different. Sometimes I sit at the bar for hours talking to him about art and the artist. He's Jamaican, or is it Barbadian? His folks come from somewhere down there anyhow. He says he wants to be a writer, so I've kind of taken him under my wing. I even suggested to my wife, Jenny, that we invite him over for dinner.

Where is that letter? What sort of picture does he want?

I like the one of me standing before an angry sea, with a camera dangling from my wrist. A clever comment on the futility of art. But my Bermuda shorts look quite silly.

Perhaps this one: autumnal, frowning, in front of our first house. Too bourgeois.

– Honey, where's that photo of me strolling through the colonnade at the Louvre?

That was a mistake. Five days later I find a better one, a shot of me sipping an espresso outside a streetside café one October afternoon. A black fedora lies on the table. A coy allusion. I send that one off at once, with a note stating that it should be used for my portrait instead. The Louvre shot was pretentious. (But at least he'll know I'm an art lover.) Later I phone my son, Jason, at boarding school in Oakville, and mention the good news, to which he responds with barely a grunt, tossed into the bottomless well of parental magnanimity.

I'm most attracted to Gauguin. Not so much to his work – too symbolic – but I like how he abandoned his family for Tahiti and art. I couldn't do that – Jenny and Jason, I'd feel terrible –

but I keep his temerity close to my heart, like a trap door that I'll never need to pop. For I'm hardly forty-two, and if things continue as planned I'll be retiring from stockbrokering in less than eight years.

The club: north of Queen Street, east of Jarvis, in a neighbourhood where the hookers ply their trade, it's a squat yellow-brick building that tradition keeps us from selling. Doesn't look like much but for the Mercedes and Beemers parked at the side. One night I was the last member to leave, Junior was locking up, and in the parking lot we discovered a wood-panelled minivan audibly cooling. I sneaked close: a blond, down on her knees, was hard at work on a surprisingly clean-cut john. I cleared my throat, inquired whether they were members – and then pointed to a sign on the chain-link fence:

Private Parking
Members Only

They went elsewhere.

A year ago we voted almost unanimously to put a bench by the street, to warm up the place. Alas, we did make things inviting: within days a troupe of bums had overrun the property, with their cardboard and sleeping bags. Junior chased them away, and I helped him lug the bench to the storage room in the basement, where I noticed a mounted print of van Gogh's *Wheatfield with Crows* that he'd been using for rolling fresh kegs down three steps. Giving it a wipe, I suggested he take it home, hang it in his bedroom. I told Jenny over supper, and again said that we should have him for a meal.

If I were a violent man – if I weren't in complete control of my reactions – I might slash Shitty's throat. It makes me feel better to call him that now, to his face and in my mind. We were loafing in the locker room after a shower when someone asked about my portrait.

– I don't know what's happening. I haven't heard back from Greg.

Shitty laughed.

– Maybe he took one look at your mug and decided not to paint you, even if you are Mr. *Greg Denton*. Andy and Bill guffawed.

I did not respond. I simply covered myself with my towel and went straight to my locker. That's when I started calling him Shitty.

But I am getting worried. Why haven't I heard from him? Because I sent two photos and he thinks me a fool? At the office I asked my secretary, Deirdre, to get me the phone numbers of any Greg Dentons listed in Guelph, but she snapped that she didn't work for only me; moreover, she had to leave early to pick up her mutt from the vet's.

– Go, don't worry about me. Go. Which she did. (Bitch.) The telephone operator was incompetent and couldn't locate a single Denton in Guelph, Waterloo, Kitchener or Hamilton, where I gave up, slamming down the receiver. I'll just have to write him a note:

Dear Mr. Denton,

Several months ago I mailed you, as requested, photographs of myself for a project of yours. Having not heard back from you, I thought I'd best confirm that these were received and that you understand that I give you my permission to paint only the second one (outdoor café in autumn, espresso, black fedora on table). If you'd kindly inform me as to the status of your work, it would be much appreciated. I look forward to our finally meeting.

Yours truly,

Greg Denton

That was four months ago and I'm going mad. I don't so much as mention art for days at a time, for fear of someone asking after my picture. But when Shitty goes to MOMA, in New York, it's clear I must do something lest my authority and primacy in the field of art should slip. I tell them I must leave town for a sitting, and hole up at home for three days. On the fourth I emerge victorious, announcing that Greg and I got along like a charm, he kept me for three days – my portrait is life-sized and well under way. Shitty, just back from the Big Apple, scowls into his mug of beer.

One week later I take a personal day, leave a message at the club and drive to Guelph (via Oakville, exchanging my Beemer for Jason's bohemian Beetle). At the gas station on the outskirts of town, the attendant has never heard of Greg Denton, nor of Cobbled Lane, but we inspect a road map and he highlights our findings. Before leaving, I take a good long look at myself in the bathroom mirror.

Guelph's a picturesque city, a university town. I've been here before and always found it unremarkable. But today it's transformed, Greg Denton imparting depth and substance. I press on Beethoven's Fifth and aim for the stone belfries on the horizon.

What more could a man want? A narrow lane, a cobblestone lane, quintessentially laney. Garrets atop, surely. Stone buildings shoulder each other up the hill and block the sky. When the first movement of the symphony is finished, I slide out of the car seat and slam the door with a flourish, confirming the tilt of my black beret in the glass. The building marked '11' has a rock-solid red door that sends my knuckled attack shuddering back through my body but produces hardly a sound. One of several buttons on the door frame reads, 'Apt#2GregDenton.' I press it several times, to no effect, and end up idling in the car for hours.

He finally appears six Fifth Symphonies later, a long black coat, black hair unruly, with the introspective air that marks the artist. I get out and extend my hand:

– Mr. Greg Denton, I presume.

– Ah, no, sorry. He backs away. Wrong guy, pal.

My face burns when I think about fashionable artistes. Frauds. I sit on the front steps of the building, my head buried in my hands, until an enormous iron-haired woman barges past. I crowd her on the landing and spook an answer:

– He's got a red beard and a jolly red face. *Slam.*

Red beard, okay, like Vincent. But a jolly face? I switch off Ludwig to brood in silence, anticipating the worst.

Greg Denton? The guy looks nothing like van Gogh. But it's got to be him. Unfazed by a close shave between my door and a rude cyclist, I tumble out of the car and call:

– Greg Denton, I presume!

– Yes? His eyes twinkle, and he gives me a crafty smile.

– I'm Greg Denton too.

– Hmm.

– Did you get my photographs?

He inspects me carefully. My palms are sweaty.

– Yeah, I did.

– What about the letter?

– Letter?

– I sent instructions that you paint me at the streetside café, in autumn, with that black fedora.

Again, that crafty smile, a bit wider this time, kind of talking out one side of his mouth, barely moving his teeth:

– Yeah, I got that.

– Oh, good. Okay, well, I just wanted to confirm, since I didn't hear back from you. I was worried you didn't get the photographs, but you did and you know what to do, so that's fine. Good.

He nods a tight-lipped grin, twinkles again and holds out his hand:

– So you'll receive your invitation to the opening sometime next fall.

My invitation!

– When's it going to be, and where, can I see my painting now, question mark? I give him a wry smile.

– No, I'm not showing them to any of the Gregs until then.

Junior's a letdown. Those pretentious thick-rimmed glasses he's taken to wearing. Putting on airs. He practically bit off my head when I strongly urged he read Dickens. He simply hasn't the cultural wherewithal to become a writer, yet he won't take advice and learn. I practically have to shout to get a beer now. He spends all his time text-messaging his new girlfriend and admiring his sneakers. I give up! I rescind my offer of a meal.

It took six long months of same old, same old, but this morning my invitation finally arrived. I'd told Jenny to call me on my cell as soon as it came, even if she was in doubt, and twice I battled traffic home to tear into a free fitness membership and then an invitation to resubscribe. But I didn't anger. I just steeled myself for Shitty's snide remarks. But this morning, a third call from Jenny: an envelope with an art-gallery logo is here. I flicked Smitty with a wet towel and howled at the thought of him cursing as I motored home.

Yes, September has been good to me. The first week Fred, the president, frowning, told me Junior had given notice; the third week Junior left; and now my invitation:

Dear Mr. Denton,

Enclosed is the invitation for my upcoming exhibit, *Greg Denton, I Presume …* , opening November 11th at 8:00 p.m. I would very much appreciate your attendance. All the Greg Dentons will be assembling in the back of the gallery at 7:30. We'll do a toast, I'll have an opportunity to thank each of you, and then shortly after 8:00 we will join the crowd in the front for the first viewing of your portraits. Thank you again for your co-operation. I look forward to our meeting.

Yours truly,
Greg Denton

I'm completely overwhelmed. I did not expect this special treatment – to say nothing of having inspired the name with my impromptu salutation! I go straight back to the club, but Smitty's gone, so I show the letter to the new guy behind the bar (Mack, also black). He looks, and a couple minutes later I read it aloud, with emphasis, to be sure he understands the exact significance and will report it accurately. Finally, like some secret we've both been waiting for me to share, I draw the official invitation from my pocket and slide it over the counter toward him. On the cover, a black square, nothing else; and inside, in great bold letters, 'Greg Denton, I Presume...' Mack looks at me uncertainly, but we cackle together when I imitate Greg's crafty smile and tell him exactly how the name came about.

I admit (not to Mack), I did lodge a complaint against Junior. His inattention and increasingly blatant rudeness kept going unnoticed by the others, who never paid him any mind, so I had to be creative. The harmony of our club was at stake.

– It pains me to tell you this, fellows. I think Junior's become a bit light-fingered.

– You mean he's stealing? Fred asked. He was sitting up on the top bench in the sauna. I'd gotten stuck down below. Is that what you mean, Greg?

I nodded.

– Stealing what?

– Well, for one thing ... I detailed the rather fine van Gogh print that had gone missing from the storeroom.

– That thing? Is it yours?

I shook my head.

– The club's?

– That's right.

An awkward silence. Someone splashed water on the rocks – *hissss* – and Fred, increasingly shrouded, gave Andy, beside him, one of those raised-brow, you-can't-trust-anybody-these-days looks before he disappeared in the thickening steam.

– I think we can let this one slide, I heard him say.

A hot, white period of wordless reflection ensued.

But Junior became intolerable. Somebody must have said something about my finger-pointing, because he'd glare at me, no matter where I sat. Afraid he was becoming dangerous, I took certain precautions, not using the showers alone, always sitting with another member, *never* being the last to leave at night. Mack's appearance was the best thing that could have happened. I even considered inviting him to the opening. But luckily I remembered, in the nick of time, that the invitation was addressed to me only. Already I was hoping to sneak my wife in.

I made a list:

1. Explain to Jenny that she should come, but there's the off chance she'll have to wait in the car.

– You're kidding, Greg. You are nuts. He's not Jackson Pollock.

– Honey, I'm just warning you, the invitation is addressed to me only. I can't be sure that Greg will let you in.

– I'm your wife! If he doesn't let me in, I'll run the car through the gallery window.

She wouldn't do that. But an embarrassing scene, maybe. I phone the gallery at once.

– Hi, you've reached Agora. We're presently showing *The Nutcracker*, a Veronica Stern demonstration, until November 1st. Greg Denton's *Greg Denton, I Presume…* opens November 11th and hangs until January 5th. Feel free to leave a message at the tone. *Beeeep.*

– Yes, this is a message for Greg Denton: Greg Denton here, in Toronto. I've just received my invitation to the opening and am very much looking forward it. But I just wanted to check whether or not my wife could come. If you could call me back, it would be much appreciated. Thank you.

I pick up the receiver one last time at midnight, just in case, and to my surprise there's a message: Bring whoever you want.

– It's settled, you can come, I tell Jenny as I hop into bed. She rolls her eyes and rolls over.

2. Study the invitation from Greg's last exhibit and prepare an aesthetic critique.

– Deirdre, would you mind slipping down to the plaza to make me some colour copies? I'll tape one to my desk, one beside the bathroom mirror and one in my locker. I'm also generating a list of keywords – *impasto, chiaroscuro*, etc. – and I plan to memorize the following: ' … the improvisational and the predetermined resonate with the status of these portraits as possible depictions of the individual on one hand, and depictions of the dissolution of the individual – an alleged postmodern predicament – on the other.' Rolling this statement around in my head, I try to decide what to think. I compare it to the new invite's cryptic question, 'What's in a name?', in tiny type between parentheses on the back. When Deirdre returns I ask her to photocopy this as well, but she gives me a look such as would not have been tolerated two decades ago, and snorts, 'Busy.' Sighing, I wave her out of my office.

3. Remind Jenny to get a new dress – black.

4. Decide what to wear myself. For this last item I've employed Smitty. Careful here, there's method to my madness. You see, Smitty's been to MOMA. I haven't (responsibilities, responsibilities!), and 'postmodernism' unnerves me. After all, I'm *classically* trained. But I do not want to be thought a philistine at the opening. Now don't go thinking I've compromised my advantage. Certainly, Smitty is flattered. But the stupendous fact that my portrait has been painted by an important postmodernist is reinforced with each discussion and every trip to the tailor. When the deed is done, a new suit mine, I crown my success by pulling the letter one more time from my attaché

case, conveniently forgetting that Smitty has read it. With a caustic smile, he reminds me.

I thought something staid would be best, something radical but staid. Smitty was adamant:

— Black's pretentious, you look like a phony. Try this.

Pink. Pale, but unmistakably pink. You can guess what I said:

— Forget it, Shitty. Quit your clowning. To ensure his complete co-operation, I pulled out all the stops: You and your postmodernist knowledge. Your good taste. Now help me out here.

That did the trick. What he picked out next repelled me no less than its nerve delighted me, and when I had it on I felt liberal and empowered: a bronze suit, a dark purple shirt, a bronze tie and a pair of pointed magenta shoes. *Yes.* I was carefully measured, and a few days later picked it up, went to the club and showed Cam and John, who both agreed, it's hip. Smitty and I picked it together. I know my colours.

ॐ

— Why didn't you tell me, you brazen dingbat? says Jenny, laughing. You're lucky I've got a red dress in the closet.

I knew I forgot something: namely, Item #3 should have been revised when I decided what to wear. But she looks good when she reappears, and we look good together in the mirror. I don't remember feeling this proud maybe since we got married. My bronze picks up soft accents from her red and reflects a fulsome tan all over her. I check out my three-day beard, and while Jenny paints her face, I comb in some of Jason's hair gel. Finally, I slip on those pointed magenta shoes, using Dad's famous silver shoehorn, and we toast with champers – *To Art* – before heading to Oakville to borrow the funky Beetle.

Things have a funny way of working out. The Beetle got a flat midway between Oakville and Guelph. Jenny paced, while I cursed the jack and flat and all the bad luck that seemed bent on me, when my tie somehow flipped into the screw mechanism and tugged me down so that I banged my head. Well, the tie was ruined, grease threaded into the sheen, crushed and frayed. I badly dented the hood of the car with the jack handle, and the door as well, but we had to move if we were going to make it, so I changed that fucking tire and we were off.

But as I say, sometimes things happen for a reason, and not even Greg Denton is wearing a tie. Nope, jeans and a casual collared shirt, which at first took me aback, and perhaps I was a little more reserved than usual, at the back entrance when he shook my hand. I might have been embarrassed if I hadn't already known him, if I hadn't recognized that rocking smile that looked me up and down and said, 'Nice suit,' like hilarity was all on his side. But I'm onto Greg and I've practiced my own crafty smile, drawing out one side of my mouth more than the other and nodding with an ironic air, which is how I responded when he sized up my suit, and we shared a look and a superior laugh.

Inside, the Gregs are standoffish. Most wait with wives or alone, muttering and dipping into sparkling wine like hyperstimulated hummingbirds. When Greg introduces me and Jenny (with a bullhorn!), they glare and smooth their shirts:

– Ladies and gentlemen, I'd now like to introduce Greg and Jenny Denton of Toronto. Greg's a stockbroker, and he does a little painting on the side. Wonderful to have so many painters here. He hands us each a plastic cup.

So we're released into the room, and because I've already got a relationship with Greg, with whom I feel a certain parity thanks to my unacknowledged role in naming the whole project, I start confidently introducing myself to some of the others and trading data: Father of Five, 'Writer,' Unabashed Homosexual – enough already. These guys are way underdressed, the only suit, a salesman. We fix our position beside a burgundy velvet curtain, and I assume a haughty expression when another unwanted Denton gets announced.

At five to eight Greg makes a speech:

– How marvellous to have ten of my eleven subjects here tonight. Thank you for trusting me with your images, and for coming and adding so many dimensions to this opening. Most of you I've met or spoken with at least once, some quite a number of times. But no one has seen his portrait. It's a very exciting evening for us all. I have a final favour to ask before I present you to the audience on the other side of this curtain: on that table, over in the corner, are pens, paper and a locked box. I beg you to take a few moments before you leave tonight to write a response to your portrait, to the exhibit as a whole, to both if you like. Write whatever you want. You're going to notice on each picture frame a brass plate with a number. Later, I'll remove these and engrave short excerpts from your respective responses, to be screwed back on. If you don't respond, your portrait will read, 'No Response.' Again, thank you for your participation. The paintings will hang here for two months, and then elsewhere, I hope. Do come and have a look anytime. Now, please join me in a toast to our name.

He raises his glass.

– To Greg Denton.

– To Greg Denton, we intone.

– I'd like you to gather near the curtains and enter as I announce you.

With that he disappears, and we push confusedly into the curtains, feeling for where they part, until the developing crisis finds its voice in Greg the Gay:

– For heaven's sake, how will we know whom he's referring to?

We grumble a bunch of *yeah*s, but a fanfare in the gallery quiets us, and we turn to the sound of Greg's important voice:

– Wow! What a great turnout. Thank you for joining us. I love doing portraits. As many of you know, these were inspired by photographs mailed to me by eleven Greg Dentons I'd never met before. All but one sent pretty straightforward pictures. All but one are here tonight. And they're about to see their portraits for the very first time. So without further delay, let's show them what I made of them.

All together, we lurch toward the opening. Those of us with wives turn to them for answers. Jenny squeezes my hand.

– I'll begin with the painting in the far right corner of the gallery. Please put your hands together for *Greg Denton, at his first art exhibit, with deep reservations.*

Gay Greg leaps back; three others push forward, stop and regard one another, each asserting that the Greg announced is him. Soon Greg's red face pokes through the curtains, looks them up and down and disappears again.

– I'm sorry, folks. *Greg Denton, at his first exhibit, with deep reservations and a sturdy wooden cane.*

A small grey man I hadn't noticed hobbles through the curtains to loud applause. We blush and press forward.

– Proceeding clockwise, *Greg Denton was the best goalie the Townsville Fliers ever had.*

A short beard with a belly struts forth, beaming, his clapping wife in tow.

The introductions continue unrelentingly and I don't know what to listen for but secretly await, *Greg Denton, Painter.* Imagine telling Smitty.

– Greg Denton, painter – I step forward *– of innumerable rooms, in neutral tones.* I stop. That's not me. Has he mixed me up? An ashen face floats grimly past and I sigh with relief.

– Greg Denton dons golden threads in anticipation.

It's Jenny's whoop that identifies me. I shove the others aside and emerge through the heavy curtains into a red spotlight shining down on my right and another red on my left. Directly in front of me is an enormous – I'd say five times life-size – portrait of Greg Denton, our painter. But the perspective's distorted: the face, treated super-realistically, is crushed into two-dimensionality as though up against a sheet of glass, while the smocked torso and arms are blurry but done with three-dimensional effects. One unfocused paw holds up a paintbrush with a long, tapering red handle that comes into flat clarity across the face, the brush itself lost in a bunch of red hair. In the background of the painting a counterpoised naked backside with hard, bulbous buttocks is reflected in a mirror, as are curtains like the ones behind me.

Catcalls and cheers erupt from the crowd. Greg guides me into the spotlight to my right, and I start seeing people I know: Smitty, in a black suit, bobbing around in front of me – 'Hah, Greggo, yeah!' A man bearing an uncanny resemblance to my long-dead granddad, with his mottled nose and shedding cigar stump. And there, in a far-off corner, is that Junior, plotting with Mack? Walls of faces successively part as I press ahead in my knowing way, gripping Jenny's hand – 'It's all right, my dear, everything will be fine' – until a pocket of space opens directly in front of us: my portrait. Already another Greg is loudly introduced behind us.

My portrait has a heavy, dark, wood frame and the background is flat and geometric, just like the ones on either side of it. But I've come off dynamic and sophisticated. There's Greg the house painter in ugly monochrome. The homosexual to my right has strange, distorted eyes that make me dizzy. But I sit outside the café – well, at a café-like table anyhow – wearing my black fedora for posterity. I smile and muse upon time, upon a descending line of increasingly great-grandsons marvelling at this noble ancestor, but my reflections are interrupted by Jenny's shifting around.

– I can't make out your face very well. Is it the lighting or the painting?

– Hmm, I hadn't noticed. I angle myself around, accidentally blocking the crazy portrait to my right until I'm shrieked at. It's true, my features are somewhat obscure.

– Is the paint too shiny, Greg?

I reach out to touch but catch myself.

– No, it's the fedora. I think the fedora's casting a shadow. She noses in close.

– Oh, it *is* a shadow from the hat, she says.

What the hell did he put the hat *on* me for? I nudge Jenny aside to have a look myself. Sure enough, Denton botched my face. A textbook example of poor technique – of failing to render true individuality – dressed up as an artistic mannerism. Even the shadow is badly executed, too dark, too flat, too glossy. He probably tried to fix it fifty times.

I'm disappointed, but I remind myself that I knew from the get-go Greg Denton was no master. Chiaroscuro is so difficult. But once you see a problem, you can't take your eyes off it, and suddenly my entire portrait's ruined by that damn black smear. With a protracted crafty smile to my left, I eventually catch the house painter's attention and ask what *he* thinks of my portrait. But he only glances and shrugs before he's back with his own, checking god-knows-what from all the angles, analyzing a picture so grim I feel a bit better even before Smitty sneaks in behind me with this telling slip-up:

– So are you going you buy it?

I can't resist a smile.

– What, the whole set?

– I mean, it's an exact likeness, except for the face.

– Because Greg would never break a set, you know. Artists *never* do that, unless they're desperate.

– It must be dizzying. Do you feel like you're looking in a mirror?

– No, probably it will end up at an institution – a museum or an important gallery.

– Or maybe we could get the boys to chip in for it. We could hang it next to the past presidents, in the snooker room.

Shheww, right over his head!

The crowd behind us has started jamming together on the far side of the gallery, determined, it would seem, to witness anyone and everyone catch his first glimpse of himself. Now the bullhorn again! Will it never end?

– Ladies and gentleman, one Greg Denton has not joined us tonight. My most challenging subject. Let's gather around his portrait.

Excuse me? This inordinate attention given to a guy who didn't even bother to show I find galling. Like a bunch of sheep we follow Denton into the corner, where a black sheet hangs over something on the wall. He waits for us to settle down, and speaks again:

– I can safely say there's something of all of us in Number Eleven, as I like to call him. This subject, in response to my letter requesting his picture, sent me a bunch of cut-up pieces of photos, presumably of him.

How absolutely cliché. I roll my eyes, thinking of 'dissolution of the individual – a supposedly postmodern predicament,' and try to catch Greg's attention. But he rambles on, refusing to denounce such shameless attention-seeking, fuelling my suspicion that he's a second-rater. A dauber. A fraud. Well, I agreed to help him out and I've done so. I wash my hands of the outcome. Blah, blah, blah, not enough to finish the piece, took the liberty of cutting up your images.

Excuse me? Cutting up my images?

– What did he say, Jenny?

– Shh.

– But what did he say?

– It's a pastiche, Greg. He made a pastiche of this Greg Denton out of everyone else's photos. Just listen.

– … and you ten fleshed him out.

He tugs off the sheet.

– Voilà!

Jostled on all sides, I force my way in and examine it carefully for evidence of me and my pictures. The guy looks like a leper and a schizoid. I guess the last laugh's on him, although it makes you reflect on how subjective this whole thing is. What the hell could a complete stranger like Greg Denton presume to say about any of us?

– Greg, there's your hat, says Jenny, pointing at the crap on the wall.

– Where?

– And look, your mouth.

– You've got to be kidding. My hawk-eyed wife. Christ, my mouth looks like an infected wound. Sliced off my face, put to his self-serving purpose, it's incredible it's still so distinctively mine. I'm shoved to the side without locating my hat, but I've had enough. I have the feeling you get when a stock you're heavily invested in tanks.

– Let's go, I say to Jenny, and go scrawl, 'Histrionic; a tad sophomoric; problematic handling of chiaroscuro,' on the paper marked GD 5.

Distance

'If we expect further downside, the question becomes how deep and for how long? ... Do we "grind" lower, frustrating everyone into submission (water torture) or does something happen to cause the players to "throw in the towel" (i.e., panic dumping at any price)?'

— Keith Edwards, Technical Analyst

'I ndustry is a world in itself. And this world … is in fact the largest of the planets which make up our system': Henry Luce, founder of *Fortune*, the first magazine I subscribed to as an adult. And with a Master's in economics and a talent for abstraction, soon I joined the employ of one of the top broker-age houses in the country, to tackle that world, albeit at several degrees of remove, in the role of Market Analyst. A technical analyst, properly called – or chartist, if you prefer. Alert to rumour, yet skeptical almost to a fault, driven by the age-old longing to tease patterns from life. And if my charts and indices didn't entirely do justice to its complexity – any more than a map does to a continent's, or an x-ray to a cancer's – I nonetheless believed they were visions truly glimpsed. Desk and floor space heaped with reports, reams of raw tracking data, towers of coffee cups, until – *eureka!* – an exhaustion gap, maybe, auguring the end of a stock's decline, hopefully, when the market will rally and start the share price on the uptrend of an ascending triangle.

I'd resurface from my ocean of stochastic delight, after what seemed an eternity, and hand our secretary a pithy report, to be copied, distributed and considered at length.

So what made me, of all people, even enter the Scarlet Cata-comb? Was it boredom? Dissatisfaction? An errant longing? Something like that. Keep in mind this was only a few months after the Events of September 11th, and my spirits kept on sink-ing with the bearish market. Of course, everyone had turned to me for advice – like during the dot.com crash of 2000 – so in that sense I was feeling fine, rethroned and hopeful of pulling a rabbit from my hat. But the pressure was unbearable, really, and my own portfolio was bleeding rather badly. Had I not, uncharac-teristically, had a couple of drinks with a fellow chartist before heading for home, I feel certain I would have slunk right past.

'What're you drinking, mister?'

Greatly embarrassed, I ordered a Scotch and soda without making eye contact, and was watching for her return when I noticed, on the other side of the room, to the left of the stage where stripping was transpiring, a different server, peculiarly attractive, with smooth ebony hair and muscular calves.

'That'll be eight-fifty. Want a tab?'

Yes, yes, I nodded.

She *so* resembled my wife, Gillian: even the slightly elongated face, now turned in my direction; the small, friendly mouth that took orders; the not insubstantial hips and rear as she made for the bar. Beyond that, a certain languor, which Gillian has none of, and which seemed born of a bit too much experience, or perhaps a drug problem, conspired with her scanty white outfit and shameless place of work to produce in me a hunger of uncommon intensity. Transfixed, I belted down my drink and made to move to her section, but 'Want your bill?' arrested me. Fine, fine. Hawk-eye. I paid and left, feeling dumb.

Meanwhile, my mother was at me again.

'I'm worried about you, Trevor.'

Sighing, I lowered the volume on my headset. 'Why's that?'

'A mother knows.'

'Knows what?' I careered onto the expressway.

'Stop it! What's the matter?'

'Nothing is the matter.'

'Just like Monica would say when –'

'And Mon's fine now.'

'Don't tell me you're fine. We never see you.'

'We saw you three weeks ago.'

Silence.

'Are you there, Mum?'

'You're keeping track, are you?' That tortured tone.

'No, it's just you said –'

' – – your duty – – – might – – us.' I was under an overpass.

'Hello?'

'… you – us?'

'What?'

'I said, y– '

'Hello?'

They're the ones who pushed me out. I saw no reason to leave my boyhood room until it was time to marry, but at their insistence I had my own place within months of graduation. And loved it, ensconced in that basement apartment, thinking, which of course got them worrying.

Mark this: I never accepted a lap dance. Parsimony and restraint are organic to my being. Without practical, selfless reasons, I couldn't have justified wasting time in that hole. No, it was for Gillian's sake more than mine that I kept going there. For our sex life had faded to naught, after, what, only two years of marriage? Of course she was inclined to discuss it, to 'get to the bottom of the problem.' Aren't they always? But simply scratching the surface was like nails on a blackboard for me, ending the conversation right there. With one copulation every two weeks, I kept her complaints at bay.

Yes, our sex life skyrocketed – if that trope is understood to mean the steep slope of my libido as it peaked on Sunday nights when I rushed in from the Catacomb ('Hmm, squash sure gets your juices flowing, Trev'), then slumped, slaked, fit to be forgotten for another week.

One noon hour, some weeks after I first strayed into the Cata-comb, I was lined up at the Super Happy Chinese counter in Commerce Court, trying to shake a financial adviser who was grilling me about the stability of the greenback. 'It's in my report,' I said, annoyed that he obviously had not read it very closely. My shrimp chow mein was taking forever. Tapping my toe, periodically rotating ninety degrees, when – Monica? She was supposed to be in Tofino. My sister, Monica, four years my senior, ambling toward me. That's right, ambling, impossibly at home in a crowd, scanning the faces as though at any moment she might spot a familiar one. I stepped behind a column and watched. Her baby had been born already? No, I'd have heard. I'd been intending to return her calls …

My would-be sister shed her likeness in the green glow of the Super Happy sign: what I'd taken for curiosity was in fact a nervous, erratically flickering glance. She trod past and into virtual sisterdom again.

'Shrimp chow mein!'

Incredible, I marvelled, following her across the food court with my tray. I sat at a table inconspicuously facing hers. Even the way she ate, picking through her carton of fries with a fork.

She was almost finished, contemplatively nibbling a crisp one, when a silent blob of ketchup slipped onto her lapel. Then back to the carton to root. Done, dab, dab, the corners of her mouth. Out came her pocket mirror.

I hate seeing people preparing to engage – raising ramparts. Once I stumbled on my dad nodding at himself in the bath-room, with an intent look in his eyes. We both blushed. Now this familiar stranger coloured, contoured and blotted her lips, and rose to leave. There's me, wanting to stop her. That stain on her lapel. Instead I punched a reminder into my Palm Pilot to phone Monica, soon.

Gillian's an academic. Her immensely successful doctoral thesis, *Anxious Mosaicists: Self-Definition in Toronto's* WASP *Community, 1970–1990*, was picked up for a special report by the CBC and ultimately landed her a tenure-track position at our alma mater, the University of Toronto. Her jet-black hair rains straight as arrows down past prominent cheekbones and a slightly aquiline nose.

I'm a history buff myself. A student of the bourgeoisie. My favourite period: the High Middle Ages, before the Plague. Here's to moneylenders, furriers, coopers and barbers, the Smiths, the Millers and the Taylors, for their flight from the field into lath and plaster boroughs, setting up home above their shops. Savouring mulled wine by the fire, I reflect, *These* are my people, the girded bridge to modernity. How we've burgeoned! Bankrupt nobility, swarms of peasants, the nebulous proletariat, with its disappointing aspirations: Welcome, brothers, to prudence.

But in truth, I was *living* in the past, ignoring rumours, as unsettling as biological determinism, that our models of market behaviour are, simply stated, wrong. Like everyone, I employed an arsenal of statistical tools to study risk, and never questioned why virtually every situation required adjustments to the basic procedures. Markets, I assumed, are mercurial like the mind and will never be reduced to unchanging mathematical facts. Hence the art of our profession.

Look at it this way: we all *knew* markets move to a song of emotional turns, from whimsy to greed to outrage and fear, to faith to love and back again; yet the theory behind our every calculation blithely assumed transactions reflect purely rational assessments of value.

Back at the Scarlet Catacomb. Intent on my wifely charmer, over and above less furtive appreciation for whatever was being revealed onstage. The strippers soon learned to skirt my table: no matter how they shook, I proved a barren money tree. Unfortunately, the object of my affection found me fruitless too. For at close range her grin was coarse, and she had hollow, acned cheeks. The limitations of reality. Seated just *outside* her section, I kept the mirage alive, ordering doubles until midnight, when I'd fly home, to pollinate my wife, quickly, before domestic associations dampened my enthusiasm.

Mind you, our marriage was perfectly fine. She's my only real friend, and certainly I had no intention or desire to submit myself to the ridiculous shuddering and shaking of intercourse with anybody else. Perhaps safest would have been to simply let my senses progressively dull, but what kind of a husband would that make me? Here was a way to reverse the downtrend (which, according to the stats, is practically inevitable in long-term partnerships), a model for marital regeneration, whereby an unexpected longing without any rational explanation or even any actual, touchable object could be leveraged to revitalize our 'passion,' and with a minimum of deceit. The stench of smoke and booze could be attributed to post-'squash' socials, the sudden enthusiasm for squash could be attributed to stress at work, and stress at work needed no explanation. Soon Gillian took to singing in the shower, especially after I switched to those head-numbing doubles.

Next thing you know: 'Why don't you play more often?' and 'I'd like to learn.'

'It's a men's club, hon.'

I'd have disported myself morning, noon and night just to make her happy, but I was smart enough to balance the expedient of jump-starting my libido against the risk of exploding it into something much messier and less contained than I could easily manage. Early on, I tried to pull off a second visit in one week, but suddenly lashed out at the secretary's time-consuming explanation of some trifling error she'd made and then found myself literally salivating over my manager's tapping open-toed shoe. Only when I was back in my own office, checking the Catacomb's lunch menu online, did good old-fashioned bourgeois self-restraint step in and regain control of me. Once a week was the most it could be. Still, Gillian predicted a longer, happier life for us both.

One Sunday every summer my parents have a special family barbecue. It used to be that grandparents and sundry aunts, uncles and cousins came over, and we'd set up a tottery badminton net back by the mock orange. Now all but Nan are gone from that generation, cousins are spread thin, and uncles and aunts have by and large retired to the country. Only the nucleus sticks together. Pessimistic forecasts abounded when Monica went to Victoria, a few years ago, for her Master's, even more of them when she married Clarence Bubchuck and they moved to Tofino to open that outdoor sporting-goods store of theirs.

'This should be the last, I think,' said my mother, glumly absorbed in the surface of her wine.

I protested that Gillian and I weren't going anywhere.

'Oh, it's not important to you.'

Before I could refute her, Monica piped up: 'Sandy' – since the end of high school she's been calling them, jarringly, by their first names – 'we'll be back, we promise.'

Dad reappeared from snuffing out the barbecue: 'Now, now, we've got plenty of happy summers in store.'

This year was different – Monica and Clarence's baby had arrived. Mum looked so happy, bouncing the squawker under our shuddering mountain ash. With annoyance, I observed her glancing at Gillian. Nan, on the other hand, contented herself with merely watching the child, cryptically refusing to take it, even though Monica kept thrusting the bundle at her all afternoon, between countless bald feedings.

After a terrific mess of steaks, tomatoes and fresh corn, it's tradition that everyone at the double-length picnic table make a speech, beginning with my father and proceeding clockwise. But Monica beat him to the punch when she leapt up and cried, 'I love you all so much,' in a voice cramped with incipient tears. 'Our little Benjy …' She held him up to face Dad, whom he's named after. 'Ben, he's as perfect as you.'

Averting his eyes, Dad smiled.

'Oh, Sandy, you're so … wonderful! And the best cook in the world. Clarence has been talking about your potato salad since last year.'

Mum waved at the baby.

'And Trevor. Trevor and Gillian, when are you coming to visit us?' she said, bobbing Benjy's head like he was doing the asking. Mum frowned, but caught herself.

Meanwhile, I'd been wondering, are these superlatives necessary? But with Monica's barrage of affection directed at me, I fast-forwarded through the coming months and confirmed we had no time for a visit.

Red-maned Clarence was next at the plate. He cleared the tangle from his face and made some appreciative noises. Avoiding one another's eyes, we clapped.

My turn. Hemming and hawing, I peered around, and eventually focused on Monica. 'Mon …' My mind was blank. The table was cluttered with paper plates and condiments. 'Mon, I've been intending to call.' My smile felt bony and false. 'Your lad's just beautiful.' Wooden words, knocked out in panic. Helpless, I shifted to my mother: 'Mum …' Her eyes looked suddenly so bright. 'Lunch was terrific, as always.' I raised my empty cup.

Before we left, Dad and I had a chance to talk about investing, which was nice. He had asked me to look into a stock that had been paying rather well the past few quarters. The results were promising, but I opened with a word of caution, since, really, as a periodontist, he was out of his depths. 'Be careful, Dad. There's a lot of noise in the markets right now. You were right to bring this to me.'

'What do you think? To my eye it's pretty volatile.'

'Implied volatility is high, but so's everything these days. Look, I tracked it back two years. Volatility is low. Projected earnings are good and getting better. Relative strength is outstanding, no problem there. I put together this package for you.' I snapped opened my briefcase. 'The whole gamut.' Two fat envelopes stuffed with charts, analyses and my best advice on how to proceed. 'Have a look and get back to me.'

'Why do people always tell each other they're the most this or the best that?' I asked Gillian on our way home in the car. 'It only makes things awkward.'

'That's how we express our love. Nobody takes it literally.'

'I guess.'

'Besides,' she added a few minutes later, 'it's subjective. You don't feel someone's the best whatever because it's been decided by an independent tribunal.'

'True.'

'That was nice what you said to Monica. Her eyes melted.' I found this hard to believe but, sick of worrying, tried to chase away the fear that she'd mistaken my awkwardness for indifference.

It's been nice to finally see you, said my mother at the garden gate, reluctant to release me. Thankfully, the Bubchucks were staying there for the night, so I didn't feel too badly about leaving. And later Dad would show everyone the package I'd made for him and Mum.

'Why don't we plan a trip to see them in August?'

'All the way out there? I'm not sure that's necessary.'

She slapped my arm. 'I know it's not necessary, dingbat. It would be good for both of you. For me as well. I want to get to know them better … and my *nephew*.' She laughed. 'Isn't he adorable?'

'A cute kid.'

I'm told I won't truly understand love without engendering one myself. But lord, that's a risky undertaking. Gillian kept circling around this issue for the rest of the ride, until finally she struck as I was unlocking our front door: 'Trevor, when are we going to have a baby?'

'The last goddamn thing I need right now is someone more to love.' I hurried in to deactivate the alarm, and when I turned back, she wouldn't look at me. She dropped her purse on the boot mat, wearily climbed the stairs and – despite my several, increasingly comprehensive apologies – shut herself inside the bedroom.

Alone in the den, with our plasma screen booming, I debated whether or not to play 'squash,' while a flash summer storm must have torn past, all those broken branches I later found lying in the street. Well, I concluded at the end of the movie, how else does she expect to conceive a child?

Gone for a match, honey. There's manicotti in the freezer. xox Trevor.

Knots of activity. For the first time in five months, the best tables in the Catacomb were all occupied, and the second-rate ones as well, by a bunch of jocks in football jerseys. So I was forced to sit either in the heart of my wifely server's section or so far away I'd barely be able to make her out. I reluctantly chose the former.

'What can I get you?'

There was something mulish about that smile. 'A double Scotch on the rocks, please.' I didn't look up from my interlocked hands until she was a few metres away, and still she didn't much resemble Gillian, which annoyed me.

Chewing on ice, I coolly observed Thai 'twins' contorting onstage.

'Another drink?' Her breasts pressed against my back as she reached for my glass, but I wasn't finished and said so, although I wanted to order another, with more ice this time, only her attention had already strayed to the jocks, the one shouting and waving a twenty in the air. She raced over, tray pressed to stomach like armour.

He blathered in her ear and pointed to his friend, a fat fellow who looked embarrassed. She touched that one's cheek. The instigator laughed, said something else. Laughing along, she reached for the twenty. But he stopped her and spoke again. She shook her head. 'Hold on –' He dug in his pocket and found another bill. Okay? Apparently so. For forward she leaned, to allow, to my utter disbelief, the fat man a peek inside her barely buttoned blouse!

I swallowed the last of my ice. Everyone knows, strippers strip and servers serve. Her breasts were out of bounds. The obese object of her inappropriate attention just sat there, stunned; but his buddy had no such reservations and with a whoop stuffed those bills into her cleavage, thereby breaking the law, *necessitating* my split-second heroics – i.e., my leaping up (knocking over my chair in the process) to pitch my empty tumbler straight at her assailant.

Alas, straight it did not fly. My darling spun free, one breast a-swing for all to admire, and the tumbler clocked her beneath the eye. She went down.

A psychiatrist, of all things. Not a therapist, not even a psychologist, but a psychiatrist, reserved for the organically deranged. It was my lawyer, Bob MacKentire, a partner at the firm that my family traditionally uses for real estate transactions and wills, who suggested we think about insanity. In measured tones, he explained that I'd been charged with an indictable offence (Assault Causing Bodily Harm) and ran the risk of jail time. Insanity, on the other hand: a few pretrial months with one Dr. Zbigniew Nitz, a court order to stick with him, perhaps some pills. No big deal. I demurred, repeating innocence was the only plea I could abide. I'd been defending a woman's virtue! He hemmed and nodded, but ultimately shook his head. 'The girl claims nobody grabbed her.'

The good Samaritan gets the shaft.

Bob twiddled one end of his svelte blond moustache, once again hearing me out, and then vigorously unspun the twist he'd made, flattened both sides with index fingers and smiled reassuringly. 'Your employer has agreed to put you on indefinite paid health leave.'

'Oh?' When I'd called work and explained, in a general way, my situation, to my normally quite sympathetic manager, I'd found myself shunted to HR, who seemed to want to end the call as soon as it started. Their only advice was that I not come in.

'Insanity is an illness,' Bob pointed out.

'But can I not have just a therapist?'

'No, a medical doctor for a medical problem.' I continued to fuss, until he grabbed my arm and said, 'Zbigniew is something of a "legal specialist." I use him all the time.'

'Hey, now you're talking my language.' I winked. 'But only as a legal expedient.'

Bob energetically agreed.

On my way home I stopped at work to collect some papers but found them gone, and my nameplate was missing from my office. Simon Hammer, one of the partners, famous for his friendliness, took this opportunity to wheedle into my bag and appropriate my laptop. 'Just a precaution, Trevor.'

I nodded helplessly.

'We're going to be getting new machines soon anyway, pal.' He tucked it under his arm.

'And my office … ?'

'This is pretty much a coincidence,' he said, lightly kicking the empty box that awaited my attention. 'We're thinking about transforming this whole floor into an open-concept workspace, to encourage the flow of ideas. You see, Trevor, we've become far too reliant on the whimsies of individual inspiration.' He lowered his voice: 'If I had a nickel for every cockeyed scheme one of you guys cooked up after fourteen coffees and who knows how many hours bugging out at your screens … '

I rolled my eyes in feigned concordance, at a loss for words. 'Where should I put my stuff?'

'Take it home for now. When everything's settled, give us a call. In fact – hold on … ' He picked up the phone. 'Judy, can you ask security to come give Trevor a hand with his things?' He bid me adieu and left.

Down from my office on the fifty-fifth floor, the elevator dreamily dropped. A parting nod to the security guard, and I passed from our tower into the lobby of the adjacent old Bank of Nova Scotia building, where, for a mid-afternoon break from my investigations, I'd so often taken to one of the cushioned benches with a coffee. Leaning back – yes, I'd lean right back – and perhaps a gang of brokers would bark past toward the bar, or that lead-footed money manager, thumbing his cellphone, listening, thumbing and listening; then, say, two accountants, briefcases swinging in time, or some tech-support staff without ties. In and out and up and down. And me, with that distance of my own finding.

Now, as I entered the revolving door, I tried to glance back over my shoulder, like a man in flight ought to be able to do, but was spun outside too quickly by someone coming in.

How quickly this lie of my lawyer's concoction assumed a life of its own! Simon, of course, had to mind the interest of the firm: talk of mental instability in an important in-house analyst would be incendiary. But Gillian had no excuse for taking my pragmatic course of action at face value. 'Insanity,' I told her, with an ironic smile, and thought her sigh was an indication of relief. And perhaps it was, but of the desperate sort breathed when long-sufferers of elusive conditions finally learn the cause of the symptoms that have long since laid them to waste.

'Insanity,' she repeated, following me from room to room as I tried to decide where to put my box.

'Just a legal expedient. Bob's idea.'

'Trevor, I honestly had no idea.'

'About what?'

'That you've been so … troubled.' She tried to embrace me.

'Like I said, it's a legal matter.'

'Let's make an appointment with the doctor.'

I didn't contradict her further. Sticky compassion was definitely more tolerable than her ire of the night before, when she drove me home from the police station: I tried to explain, she screamed for an explanation, repeat coda, until the bedroom curtains grew light and finally she grasped what I was saying, that I'd been defending the modesty of her likeness; that I'd been smitten by this girl because she looked exactly like her, from a distance; and that her body had all along continued to be the sole receptacle of my desire. 'Is that what you're saying, Trevor, that this was for me?'

Yes, my god, that's what I'd been saying for hours.

The corners of her mouth relented. 'Oh, my poor darling.'

I shut my eyes and tried to sleep.

'Good news!' She stood in the doorway of my third-floor study.

On all fours, I peered out from the crawl space under the steeply sloped roof. 'They've dropped the charge?'

'Dr. Nitz rearranged his schedule to see you at nine the day after tomorrow.'

'I was going to call later.'

'I want to help.' She hurried over and held out her hand. 'We'll get through this, honey.'

I backed further inside. 'I'm not done in here.'

But the tyranny of sympathy had begun.

She'd come home from work bearing gifts: a book of Impressionist reproductions, a box of Slovenian black-currant juice. The first full day of my confinement she produced *Madness: A Brief History*, to give me perspective, she said, both on how minor my difficulties truly were, and on the centrality of mental aberrations to the human story. She understands my need to feel a part of the story. I was interested to discover compulsive behaviours have often been considered by-products of refinement, and it was with fresh assurance that I knotted my tie the next morning, in preparation for my first appointment. The phone rang.

'Monkey, are you okay?'

'Actually, I'm just on my way out the door.'

'I *knew* something was going on. I keep telling your father that you're much too –'

'Work is crazy right now.'

'Work? Trevor, Gillian phoned us.' *Fuck!* 'So it's not true?'

'What isn't?'

'You didn't assault the girl?'

'Of course not. Not intentionally anyhow. I was trying to hit the guy who was harassing her.'

She sighed. 'But you've been charged.'

'Wrongly.'

'Well, we stand by you. Your father and I love you so much.'

'I do appreciate that, but I really can't talk right now.'

'I just can't understand why you were even – Can't talk? Aren't you on sick leave?'

'Mummy! I'm going to see the doctor, okay?'

'Oh, good. That's good. I'll let you go then.'

'Come in, come in, Mr. Spates. Have a seat.' Through cropped grey hair, Dr. Nitz's prickly head shone. He indicated a sturdy armchair. Facing it, at an angle, was a somewhat smaller one, without arms, presumably for him, although he returned to his desk after trying to take my jacket. 'May I call you Trevor?'

I nodded.

'Call me Zbigniew, or Dr. Nitz. Which do you prefer?'

I opted for the latter.

'Shall I tell you about myself? Yes? As you know, I'm a psychiatrist …'

I frowned.

'But I'm trained in psychology too.'

'Really?'

'You are interested in psychology?'

I exaggerated my sophomoric recollections of Freud by calling the Oedipus complex obsolete.

Dr. Nitz continued: 'The organic basis for certain patterns of behaviour interests me very much, but my true passion has always been the power of the mind – to create itself, to break itself down, to adapt and effect internal changes, physical even. Science is teaching us much about the plasticity of the brain, you know.'

I kept nodding.

'Where to begin? Sometimes medication is good. Always, psychotherapy is necessary. So –' he clicked his pen '– why are you here?'

'Bob MacKentire sent me.'

'That's not why you're here.'

I gave him a significant look, intended to seal our conspiracy, but he seemed to attribute to it some other import.

'What is it you want to tell me?'

'Nothing,' I said, genuinely baffled.

He tut-tutted me with his pen and wrote something down. 'Bob said you threw a bottle at a prostitute?'

'She wasn't a prostitute, and it wasn't a bottle.'

'Oh?'

'A server at a gentlemen's club. And an empty tumbler.'

'Okay, you threw an empty tumbler at a server. Why?'

'Some men assaulted her.'

He removed his tortoiseshell glasses and examined them under the desk lamp. 'You're her lover, hmm? Jealous?'

'Jealous? I'm married. I came to her rescue.' I laboriously explained the situation, from Gillian's exigent libido downward, and he wrote like mad, continuing long after I'd finished. Finally, he put the pen down.

'Well, you're crazy.'

Thanks be to Bob! 'That was easy.' I got up.

'Just kidding! Ha-ha. Kidding. Please sit. An icebreaker.' He waved me down. 'Sit.'

I obeyed.

'Classic Freudian scenario, right? Your affection and your sex have diverged. You are repelled by intimacy. You want to love, but you're averse to love. Why? The million-dollar question.' He seemed thoroughly satisfied with me so far. 'I'd like you to take home this test and complete it for next week.' He handed me a booklet. 'The Myers-Briggs. To help us understand the sort of person you are.'

'What if I fail?' I tried to joke.

'Then we will be off on the wrong track,' he replied, apparently serious.

'How would I fail?'

'By not being honest about your responses and preferences, hmm?'

I grumbled that next week was too soon.

'You need two weeks? Too busy?'

'No, I mean once a month is probably enough to satisfy the judge.'

'Who?'

'The judge.'

Dr. Nitz smiled. 'What did Bob tell you?'

I clammed up, afraid he'd evict me.

'Just because I find his clients troubled, he says I'm in cahoots with him. No, Trevor, I'm here to help you sort out your mind. If that helps in legal matters, so much the better. Not the other way around.'

My cell buzzed as I was driving home and without thinking I answered.

'Are you okay, Monkey?'

'Mum, I'm fine.'

'What did the doctor say?'

'There shouldn't be a problem.'

'Meaning?'

'He'll support my defence.'

'He said you're ill?'

'No, I mean –'

'Did he say why?'

'It's just legal jarg–'

'It isn't like you. How long were you sneaking off and –'

'I'm on the highway. I really do have to go.'

Gillian found me in the crawl space, rearranging boxes. 'How'd it go?'

'I found my currency collection.' When we moved into this house, shortly after getting married, I packed my childhood material away and hadn't thought about it since. Now, thanks to the many windows that had opened in my agenda, my moth-balled collections – of currency, of matchbooks, of marbles – had come to light. In particular, the paper money (the finest of it from nations long since dissolved in strife).

'What did he say?'

'Who?'

'The psychiatrist, obviously.'

'Dr. Nitz. He studied psychology too.'

'Okay, what did he say?'

'Not much. I have to do a personality test for him before our next meeting.'

'He must have said something.' She was down on her hands and knees, straining to see me by the light of just one bare bulb.

'I'm scared of intimacy.'

'What else?'

'My love and my sex have diverged. Quite common in men, apparently.'

'No guff. Can he get them to converge?'

'"The million-dollar question."' My quoting fingers suspended in the air, I belted out a laugh that drove her downstairs.

Bob was insistent about witnesses. 'I think we need to change our tack. You don't have a history of mental illness, and everything about your lifestyle suggests a well-balanced, stable person. You're just not convincingly of unsound mind.'

'That's exactly what I keep telling everyone.'

'I mean, you're a model of effectiveness.'

'Thank you, Bob.'

'So, who are the people who can corroborate your story? It sounds like you were pretty heroic.'

'That's right.'

'Who can we get to testify to this? Nobody was with you?'

I felt myself blushing.

'No call for embarrassment, Trevor.' From behind his desk he smiled reassuringly. 'I'm on *your* side.' He leaned slightly forward. 'Were you friendly with any of the girls?'

'Of course not.'

'Why "of course not"? You're a good-looking fellow, likeable, a nice dresser. It's not a crime to be friendly.'

I sat shaking my head.

'Okay.' He thought for a moment. 'What about the other staff? A bartender or a bouncer that you got to know.'

'It's no use, Bob. Can't you just subpoena them?'

'They'll probably lie through their teeth. She claims she didn't even show her breasts to anyone. Why would her co-workers contradict her?'

Suddenly I felt very tired.

'You said your family has concerns about your mental health, right?'

'Just because of this.'

'No earlier incidents?'

'Nope.'

He frowned. 'Maybe if Zbigniew put you on some pills … Okay, leave it with me. Call if you remember anything.'

'Trevor, you're an INTJ.'

The test, although just a series of yes-or-no questions, had proved surprisingly tough, challenging me to differentiate my actual self from the man I try to be. Some statements I was quick to affirm: 'You have good control over temptations and desires'; 'A thirst for adventure is close to your heart.' On the other hand, 'You are strongly touched by stories about other people's troubles' prompted some serious soul-searching. To 'You often think about mankind and its destiny,' I could have answered, 'Every waking minute' or 'Never crossed my mind,' without exactly telling a lie.

'What's an INTJ?'

He moved to the chair facing mine. 'I for Introvert, N for Intuit, T for Think and J for Judge.'

I stared at him blankly.

'Let me explain. Briggs and Myers, mother and daughter, developed their test using Jung's personality typology, which classifies people according to four pairs of opposite preferences: your focus of attention will be primarily introverted or extroverted; you will gather information by sensing or by intuition; you will make decisions from what you think or what you feel; and your attitude to the outside world will be one of judging or else of perceiving. From these we get sixteen possible combinations, or personality types, although for each pair of opposites the strength of preference varies, so it is quite complex. But you are a well-defined INTJ, indeed.'

'What does that mean?'

'Well, let's see ...' He scanned the booklet. 'INTJs are organizers. They love complex challenges and abstractions, and abhor confusion. They see globally, make patterns. Tough, logical, decisive, independent, hard on themselves.'

A clean bill of health, I told myself, proud to be of such sturdy stock.

'But, Trevor, others may find INTJs difficult to get to know. They come across as aloof.'

'So we're a little standoffish. So what?' Already I felt less badly about neglecting my loved ones.

He continued reading: 'Potential areas for growth. INTJs may not have a reliable way to translate their *valuable* insight into applications that can be realized.'

That didn't apply to me, a doer, telling the boys what's up with the market.

'They may make ill-founded decisions based on idiosyncratic information.'

Again, it didn't pertain. I have a good job, a house, a terrific wife. What's more, another of our 'weaknesses' – 'fussing over abstract issues and concerns without meaning or relevance to others' – is in point of fact a strength for the technical analyst. I was waiting for Nitz to finish, ready to tell him I'd overcome INTJ's weaknesses without sacrificing the strengths, when he added, eyeing me over the top of his glasses, 'And they may, under stress, overindulge their senses.'

'No, no, my problem's not enough sensuality.'

'Then why were you visiting strippers?'

'To re-arouse myself.'

'Do you masturbate?'

'Don't need to.'

'You don't want to?'

'Nope.'

'Why did you want to "re-arouse" yourself?'

'For Gillian.' I checked my watch. Our hour was up. He shrugged and we scheduled our next appointment.

'It's just the way I am,' I told myself, ready to update my mother. After Dr. Nitz's diagnosis of the morning, I reboxed my collections, which already bored me. They didn't seem to open onto anything interesting. I stacked them back in the crawl space and sat down at the computer.

Take this jagged line and replace each straight component of it with the same jagged line, scaled down, ad infinitum: a fractal-generating procedure that produces figures exactly like price charts – and seismographs, and also plots of cerebral activity – the obvious implication being that beneath seemingly chaotic phenomena lies order. Order implies predictability, predictability equals the holy grail, elusively glimpsed that afternoon on the World Wide Web.

When Gillian's car door slammed, I'd read just enough about Benoît Mandelbrot's fractal market model to relish its theoretical potential without yet choking on the math. I ran downstairs to tell her.

Sighing, she sat down on the couch. 'How did it go with Dr. Nitz?' was all she could bring herself to ask.

'Fine.' I stalked from the room, suddenly feeling that only he and Bob properly appreciated my many undeniable strengths.

I'd have ranked with the most prolific of Victorian diarists had I risen to Dr. Nitz's challenge and kept, 1. a record of my dreams (invariably forgotten the moment I open my eyes, ordered as they are by a logic so different from my waking life that any attempt to hook into them proves as futile as trying to remember most of childhood); 2. a hot-topic diary (probing uncomfortable topics and situations – somewhat distorted by the circumstances, I'd say); 3. a sex diary (absolutely entryless – Gillian and I were reduced to chaste caresses, sympathetic and grateful respectively; and, as I've said, I'm disinclined to masturbate). In good faith I selected a journal – a handsome Moleskine – but whenever I poised my pen, a profound lethargy would drive me to the couch for a snooze without committing a word. After four weeks Dr. Nitz conceded defeat. He charged me instead with simply paying close attention to my bodily responses in certain situations. What happened if there was a message from my mother? When I thought about my sister? Did my heart pound, my stomach churn? What thoughts did I have? Did I hear voices? How did my father factor into all this? In desperation I tried to explain that these questions weren't relevant, that this was a hoax erected on a momentary slip-up. I said exactly that, and immediately regretted it – waited to be shown the door – but Dr. Nitz gently hushed me and proceeded: 'When's the first time you remember masturbating?'

'You are extraordinarily well repressed,' he told me one day.

'I know. And no neurotic symptoms.'

'That's not true.'

'Excuse me?'

'Guilt.'

'I'm not guilty.'

'You're always feeling guilty about something. You haven't called your mother back. You forgot your sister's birthday … four months ago.'

'That's not neurotic. It hurts them.'

'Aha! How long have you felt that way?'

I shrugged. 'Wouldn't you feel bad?'

'You said your sister was attacked when you were thirteen.'

'So?'

'How did that affect you?'

'Not as much as her.'

'We're here to talk about you. How did you react to what happened?'

'It was upsetting.'

'How did you feel?'

'I don't know ... bad. Scared.'

'Why scared?'

'Why anything? She was raped. Everything changed.'

'What did?'

'Dr. Nitz, everyone did.'

It's true that my guilty conscience blossomed at a young age. When I was six I cheated in a readathon, citing books I'd never read, and long after the contest ended, I'd lie awake at night, listening for the phone call from a parent who had questioned my rather long list. A dollar bill stolen from my father's top dresser drawer for an ice-cream cone bothered me for years. Sometimes I'd hurl myself into my mother's arms to repeat how I loved her, atoning without confessing. Apparently Freud attributed this sort of nagging remorse, ever circling the mind for a fresh peccadillo, to repressed desire, sexual and murderous. But for me it had to do with being exceedingly anxious to please my parents, yet peculiarly disposed to betray them. Once I learned to keep my nose clean, the worst of it went away.

This monster, this fake madness Bob and I cooked up, was beginning to drive me mad. I'd awaken in the middle of the night to a scream of sheer terror that seemed to come from some other dimension, not quite in my head. The first time this happened, I woke Gillian. I thought one of our neighbours was being attacked. She calmed me down, but then I had to lie there and listen and listen to her sobbing into the pillow. Best to not involve her again.

When I told Dr. Nitz, he nodded, with a look of grim satisfaction. 'The buried boy.'

'Or the hacked-up man.'

'Exactly, Trevor.'

Still, I wasn't entirely convinced it was emanating from me. One Sunday morning, lying in bed, I risked explaining this to Gillian.

'I don't understand, Trev.'

'It feels like something beyond me. I can't explain exactly. Like I'm tuning into some ongoing, impersonal agony outside me. It never actually stops, but can only be … heard, I guess, from a peculiar mental angle, figuratively speaking.'

'This is part of your sickness. Like Dr. Nitz said, your inner child is screaming to be heard. Listen carefully. Get in touch with your feelings. They're what make us human.'

'Human? Then what am I?'

'What I mean is you'll regain a more satisfying human experience.'

'I like my experience.'

'You're happy?'

'No, not now that I'm on health leave for insanity and you treat me like a Ming vase. But I was more or less fine before.'

'What about the stripper and all that? How do you think you got here?'

'The server was a slip-up. If people would just leave me alone, I'd be pretty much okay.'

She sighed and, with strained equanimity, said, 'I was talking to a friend in the psychology department –'

'A friend in the psychology department! What'd you tell her?'

'Nothing, no details. I had to talk to someone. Trev, it's like your spirit's trapped in a pressure cooker. When we first got together, okay, you were restrained. I love that about you. But now, you literally cringe when I try to discuss our sex life. Sometimes I feel like you're repelled by me.'

'Things are a bit complicated at the moment.'

'I'm not talking about now, dammit.'

'Aren't you forgetting that I liked that girl precisely because she looked so much like you?'

'Is that supposed to be a compliment? What's wrong with me? Should I dress up like a whore? Would that turn your crank? I'll do it, if that's what you want.'

'Okay, okay, calm down.'

She took a deep breath. 'My friend told me that some people's sheer dread of being possessed makes them repress any feelings that draw them to others. Repulsion takes the place of attraction, and they develop a very low threshold for intimacy. These people often get so mannered and neurotic, they lose touch even with themselves.'

'Listen, I haven't lost a bloody thing – except my freedom, because of this fiasco.'

She touched my heart and peered into my eyes, as purposeful as an optometrist.

'Oh, stop.' I rolled over. 'This is a joke.'

'Breathe deeply. Try to raise your intimacy threshold.'

'A bad fucking joke.' My voice sounded pinched, barely controlled. 'Everyone wants me to be something I'm not.'

'God, all we want is for you to be happy.'

Well, she certainly came up with the worst solution imaginable: a trip to Tofino, to see my sister, her husband and their blasted baby. She arrived home from the library one August afternoon with a thick hardcover entitled *The Sober Majority: Bourgeois and Democracy*, by Reynold Hass, beautifully illustrated. I'd been in my study, massaging my temples, struggling to comprehend why the fractal market model suggests risk and the probability of catastrophic loss are so much greater than classically allowed. Being isolated from colleagues should have been conducive to assimilating new ideas, but these attempts at cogitation were undermined by self-doubt as my confidence in the tools I'd always relied on corroded. Worse still, my mathematical training was proving inadequate for compassing the fundamentals of even the old system, let alone this new one. Ready for the bosom of my favourite class of folk, I cracked the book open and found two tickets for a flight to Vancouver, departing the very next day.

'But I have an appointment with Dr. Nitz.'

'I don't care.' She handed me the phone. 'Call him.' Unexpectedly, he answered.

'Dr. Nitz, Trevor Spates here. Listen …' I told him the plan, sounding appropriately exhausted. 'But I have an appointment with you and, frankly, I don't want to miss it.'

'Yes, aren't we making good progress?'

For once, I agreed.

'But no, Trevor, this trip is precisely what you need. Better than a hundred appointments with me. You must go.'

I tried to object.

'We can do next week's session over the phone. Okay?' He extracted a goodbye from me and hung up.

'Then it's settled,' said Gillian. 'Sand in your hair, wind betwee– I mean – don't worry, it will be terrific.'

We had to catch a limo before daybreak, no problem for me, for I hardly slept a wink, tormented by the thought of leaving home to trek across Vancouver Island for an onslaught of inquiry and affection, just when I should have been locking myself in my study to concentrate. I stomped downstairs at three, put on a pot of coffee and, munching toast with marmalade at the kitchen table, browsed the preface to my new book: 'The pragmatic, if self-interested, vacillations between conservatism and liberalism so characteristic of the bourgeoisie have, over centuries, absorbed many a potentially devastating shock, with the result that, like a mighty ship, the West forged slowly, steadily ahead, through storm after socio-political storm, toward liberty and democracy.' I took courage. It was going to be a very good read.

The smell of burning jet fuel always touches off this wanderlust that I don't seem prone to act on. How I love the glossy photos, in annual reports, of colourful Africans rallying around a Coke truck, of those giant Jamaican bauxite mines I cautioned our investors against, or the endless brown pampas of the Argentine that you must cross to reach the gold. All those destinations, scrolling down the screen. Perhaps someday, once my case is cleared up ...

We had seats in Executive Class, right up front, under the gracefully conducting arms of our flight attendant, Gina. Of course the front's the most dangerous part of the plane, the tail tending to snap off and spin free of the fireball, but comfort and convenience cannot but recommend themselves, and the chance of a crash is still vanishingly small. Soon came the piping-hot towels, with their tingly evaporative effect, to perk us up, brace us to face the sun, which outpaced us across the sky. (How odd, I reflected, that we aren't actually moving forward at all – taking forward to be the direction we're heading – caught up in the whirlwind of our planet, any more than a child is moving forward on one of those horizontal airport escalators when he's hopped over the rails to the opposite side, to be promptly swept away in spite of the fact he's now running as fast as he can toward his parents, as they're borne in the opposite direction, though they try with all their might to reach him too.)

Gillian fell into a noisy, rhythmic snooze the moment Gina cleared her tray. I covered her with a blanket. Then I fired up my laptop and, blowing across a cup of hot java, took a peek at some information I'd downloaded about gold mining in Zimbabwe.

I wanted to get my hands dirty – say, in the commodities market. But at ground level, grinning over a fresh batch of ingot, or giving the nod to a shipment of saffron before repairing to the verandah for a G&T. Technical analysis was starting to feel too much like chasing rainbows. But with insufficient data to reach any conclusions, I soon exchanged my computer for the duty-free catalogue, a short-lived thrill, packed as it was with merchandise substantively no different from what you find in any old department store, for a buck or two less.

'Ah, Gina …'

She was all smiles.

'I'd like to place an order for a bottle of this single-malt Scotch.' I pointed to the picture, unwilling to jam my tongue against its clotted Celtic consonants.

'Sorry, sir, duty-free is only available on international flights.'

'Of course!' I quickly found my book and flipped to chapter one: 'Money Changers in the Temple: Opportunism/ Opportunity.'

Inevitably and all too soon, as signalled by pressure that was building in my ears, our flight began descending from the firmament that had kept it aloft for however many hours. Like some mythically wingèd phallus, into Vancouver we screamed, to touch down at 10:05, their time.

They greeted us inside the airport, all teeth, waving querulous Benjy's hand for him. I'd been trailing behind Gillian's rolling bag, dragging my own, warming up my facial musculature, when I was bowled over by their polyphonic shriek: 'There you are!' 'Hi, hi.' 'Oh my god, over here! Trevor, Gillian, *here*.' They came at us full tilt, and Monica looped her arms around my neck. Next she grabbed the baby from Clarence (who had weaved his normally unkempt hair into a long, tapering braid) and shoved it in my face. I recoiled, certain I smelled feces. Then it was Clarence's turn for an embrace: he squeezed me long and hard, like a lemon he wanted to drain of its very last drop. When finally he released me, I wondered aloud where I might find a newsstand, but we were off, nattering as we went, loading our luggage excitedly into the trunk of their canary-yellow suv. They strapped me in beside Clarence.

He drove in precise accordance with the posted limit: 15 km/hr near the terminal, through 40, 60, 30 on the on-ramp, at last 80 on the outskirts of town, and down to 10 approaching the ferry queue, badgering me with questions through every minute adjustment. 'How you been?' Well. 'Hot back home in the armpit?' Not so bad, with central air. 'How's Ben and Sandy?' They're fine. 'Did they manage to get out of town?' Niagara-on-the-Lake, I believe. 'You?' Nope. Behind us the women prattled about the baby's extraordinary progress. Gillian could not believe he had so much control of his head. Finally, there was a general expression of concern about the atypicality of some recent weather events – hail, heat, drought, frost – to which Clarence added a catalogue of natural disasters worldwide, before we fell silent, at the end of a long line of convectively warping cars with engines cut but audibly ticking, waiting for the ferry to come and admit us.

I mean, it was *hot*. Not at all what I'd been expecting from rainy old Vancouver. I shut my window and reached for the A/C as soon as we left the airport, but Clarence stayed my hand, saying, 'Keep that window down, partner. Feel the coastal wind blow.' Blow-schmow. I protested that the blast was too much for the women and child in the back – he dismissed my concern with a 'Yeah, yeah.' Happily, the gale limited the scope of our Q&A.

My god, that sun was bright, and the water, glaring like a mirror. Clarence's suggestion that he and I mosey up to the top deck of the ship (every inch of which was white) to get some air was hardly inviting, so I told him I was sensitive to sun, which is true – it annoys me when it's bright. Instead, we all squeezed into a booth in the climate-controlled lounge, Clarence – still incredulous that anyone would want to be inside on such a day – stationing himself directly opposite me and sipping mint tea that he'd brought in a yellow Thermos.

He started peppering me with questions about the economic consequences of the Twin Towers catastrophe. Why was the Canadian economy still so robust? What would happen if America attacked Iraq? Apparently my views had acquired a certain relevance. Always open to converts, I spooned the excess froth off my cappuccino and asked, 'You're worried about some securities?'

'Hell, no – just curious.'

Effing tree hugger.

On the third leg of our journey from Vancouver to Tofino, in the middle of a twist on the tortuous road that corkscrews Vancouver Island from Departure Bay onward, I needed to relieve myself, urgently. I had sucked back three cappuccinos on the ferry, in defiance of Gillian's forbidding glances, and now we were in the middle of nowhere, without hope of a rest stop for I knew not how many miles. Resigned to going alfresco, I requested a stop.

'No problemo.' We pulled over.

'Look at the view,' said Gillian, referring to a perpendicular drop-off on our right.

I was eyeing the sheer cliff to our left, bristling with evergreens, dense enough to conceal me, but to gain purchase I'd have had to have Clarence outfit me with all the latest alpine gear. 'Where do you expect me to go?'

'By the side of the road, silly,' said my sister.

'But –' I turned to protest, to suggest we relocate to an easily accessible grove or a laneway, even just a patch of scrub, and saw Clarence wink in his rear-view mirror.

'I'm on the *threshold* as well.'

'Me too,' my sister replied. 'Definitely.'

Good lord! I practically had to step over them they were at it so quickly, right beside the car, squatting and prattling and spraying. Trying to seem casual, I ambled some ten or twelve metres up the road, and stood with my member in my hand, as pointless as a fountain in winter.

What's with the 'threshold' business, I asked myself, squirming in the seat as we tackled another bend. Gillian and her big mouth. Not wanting to let on that I'd failed to urinate, I announced I was going to vomit when we finally blew into a town.

'Fuck, not in the car!' He cut off a pickup and into a gas station. I bolted myself inside the filthy bathroom.

Tofino, 'a favourite haunt of hikers, surfers, whale watchers and naturalists,' was an improbable destination for me. Think

Clarence's hair writ large. I hadn't packed any suits, of course. Open to further compromise, I closeted my sports jacket upon entering their timbered home and donned a tweedy tie fit for promenades by the sea. But jacketless, I felt naked, slinking about town on my own, again attempting to evade my keepers, not stopping to examine even the flyers for whale watching taped in so many a storefront window (although I'd been thrilled to discover that whales still exist in the wild). Like an occupying force, tanned youths with toothsome smiles dominated every establishment – girls who I suppose were about my age, although their shredded attire, suggestive of a bear-watching expedition gone wrong, made me feel like a refugee from a more civilized time, who, in his flight to the bestial present, had lost his jacket, hat and polished walking stick.

My tie periodically whipping my face, I descended a lane to the wharf, to tread the docks and smile to myself, thinking about how people would respond if I left the firm and struck out on my own. I was of two minds: either keep my position, take the time and make the effort to thoroughly understand the fractal model, and then try to come up with some applications (but even Mandelbrot has yet to apply it, and he's a genius); or else take my analytical expertise and, in the first of five career changes that are said to be our fate, remake myself into a financial adviser, but one who dashes off hither and thither to examine operations and find out if the fundamentals are solid. I recalled what Simon had said about the firm moving away from individual inspiration. What would be my role there?

To Bob, on the other hand, my prospects were hemmed in by the more immediate problem of my alleged crime. At 7:30 that morning I'd had to caffeinate myself for another tête-à-tête on the improbability of the very defence he'd sold me on in the first place, this time over the phone. First he'd tried to pin me down on Dr. Nitz's findings.

'I'm extraordinarily well repressed.'

'Anything else?'

'He wishes I'd take up masturbation.'

'So you have a serious problem? Compulsive-like?'

'Not serious, I don't think, no.'

'I know from other clients that Zbigniew is an advocate of masturbation, so if he thinks you need to cut it out …'

'No, Bob, it's –'

'Surely there's an argument there for medicating. Frankly, we need to cut our losses, find you a documented condition and demonstrate that you're committed to dealing with it. Then we'll plea bargain down to common assault and maybe get you a suspended sentence.'

'No, what he objects to is that I don't masturbate at all.'

'Oh.'

'Which seems a lot better to me.'

'Well … the main thing is that we show you're doing everything in your power to overcome your condition, so if I were you I'd get after Zbigniew for a good solid prescription. And let's keep masturbation out of this. Smells a bit off, don't you agree?'

'It should never have come up in the first place.' I hung up and, with surprising ease, fell back asleep and didn't open my eyes until I could hear that breakfast was finished and the others were out on the deck. By careful manoeuvring, I slipped out undetected, and only now, in the open air, under a hazy sky, with seagulls screaming overhead, did I start to recognize the singular importance of keeping 'jail time' out of my sentence.

'You looking for something, professor?'

I looked up from the mesmerizing planks and saw, beyond one of the narrow docks that jutted out from the main one I was pacing, a head of snowy curls – a man standing in a tethered boat.

'Me?'

'How'd you like to buy a fish?'

'No, thank you.'

'Some crabs?'

I almost refused those also, but then thought what the heck, crab fresh from the sea, delivered straight into my hands by this salty mate. Why not?

'Come. Have a look.'

Uneasily, I approached – leaned to peer into the boat.

'C'mon, c'mon.' He had a disarming habit of angling his head when he spoke. Taking his hand, I stepped down, into a wide iron craft, which, it turned out, was really quite stable. 'How many do you think you'd like?' He opened a crate.

'Well, I don't know …' I eyed the ancient creatures – cramped in ice – and hoped they were good and dead. 'There are four of us.'

'How 'bout a dozen?'

Grateful for the advice, I paid a surprisingly small sum for a weighty, dripping bag. 'They're alive!'

'Just the claws.'

What that meant I wasn't sure. I only hoped the plastic would withstand their clicking machinations until I handed them off to Clarence.

'Where are you from, mate?'

I told him.

He whistled. 'Me too.'

'No kidding?'

'I grew up on Wellesley Street.'

'Right around the corner from my squash club!'

'We were fishers, Dad and me.'

'Fishers? On Lake Ontario?'

Somehow it came up that I'd never been out in a boat, other than the occasional ferry. 'Shall we go for a spin then, mate?'

'A spin? Right now?'

'Sure, just around the inlet.'

My would-be spontaneous heart warmed to the idea. 'Sounds terrific!'

'Then throw the lines.' He started the motor. 'Aren't you going to throw them?'

'Throw them?'

'Untie the boat.'

'Aha.' I struggled with the knots until he came over and, with a couple of sharp jerks, 'threw' them himself. Then we crept, in reverse, away from the dock.

'Trevor!'

The hazy sound brought to mind something deeper, like a fjord, teeming with lore. We started moving forward.

'Trevor!'

'Is that someone calling you, professor?' He pointed to the shore.

'No, no.' I waved him on.

'Yup, somebody's calling. Right over there.'

I twisted around and, dammit, there was Gillian, galloping down the hill, my cursed appellation bouncing on her tongue. 'Hold on a sec. My wife.'

He killed the motor.

'What are you doing, Trev?'

They simply refused to leave me alone. I'd tried creeping up the beach by the house, but there would be Clarence, remarking on the weather. Or I'd sneak out the side door and hurry toward town, but Gillian would catch me with a 'Where are we going?' Now I waved. 'I'm off for a little spin, my dear.'

Standing on the end of the dock, she made a visor of her hand. 'You can hardly swim.'

I jabbed my thumb to get the fisherman to proceed, at once. 'She's exaggerating.'

He merely tilted his face to meet the slightly clouded sun.

'I was just about to put on a life jacket.' I signalled for him to pass me one.

But when finally he cottoned on, what he gave me was a kind of threadbare pillow. 'This floats.'

I raised it for my wife's inspection.

'That's not going to save you. Are you craz– ?' She caught herself in the nick of time. 'Come back to shore, Trevor. Your legs weren't made for water.'

'I've got to sell my catch,' said the fisherman, glancing at his watch.

'Haven't you got life jackets?'

'I do, but …' He pulled one down from under the roof of the cabin; I waved it at Gillian and put it on.

'That's five sizes too big for you!' True, I was swimming in straps. 'What's gotten into you?'

I looked to the fisherman, who shrugged.

'Should we get you back ashore, so you can cook them crabs?' He hit the ignition and aimed for the dock, where Gillian was waiting to smother me in kisses.

But where did they expect me to flee to, those five days in verdant hell? Their property backed on the endless ocean, they could easily track me down in town, and nobody honestly believed I'd go tramping through the murky forest that hemmed us in on all sides (although I would have, if I'd found a path). What kept me from falling apart, though, was the gratifying knowledge that my incessant and often inconvenient bids for 'a breath of fresh air,' on which I'd have to be accompanied, were starting to annoy my loved ones. After breakfast on the Tuesday, for instance, our fourth and second-last day there, it was only with testy sighs that they saucered their half-finished coffees so I could take umbrage under a system of roots that had washed up on the shore the winter before. They finally conceded that neither continuous company nor the lure of that noisome child was going to break the back of my uncommunicativeness: Clarence was charged with a direct assault.

That afternoon I began sipping Scotch at five, having been dragged out onto the deck to watch storm clouds cramp the horizon, and I continued non-stop through supper – surprisingly, without any objections. So when Clarence approached me in the rocking chair, by the fireless wood stove, I was sufficiently sedated to stay put.

'You'd like a brandy.' He handed me a snifterful and sank into the couch with a mug of camomile. 'I hear you've been having problems.'

'Oh, well, things are much better now.'

He touched my knee. 'What's going on, Trevor?'

'Nothing, really. Actually, I'm at a turning point.'

'Oh?'

'Yes, I'm ready to make some changes.'

'Really?'

'I came across this revolutionary theory about market dynamics, and it got me thinking –'

'Trevor!' He jumped up to pace between the stove and screen door, beyond which the ocean kept crashing. 'We are not here to talk about your work.' He sat and, through that rat's nest, tried to fix my eyes. 'I do understand where you're coming from.'

'How so?' I coolly replied, unable to imagine what that lazy schmuck could possibly understand about my passionate interests.

'Did you know that I'm an alcoholic?'

'Excuse me?'

'I used to start with bourbon in my morning coffee and by

noon – I worked in a bike shop in Victoria – would already have the better of a forty pounder.'

'Clarence, I never would have …' I loosened my tie. 'What made you stop?'

'I met your sister.'

'That simple?'

'Well, not quite, but I met her – she came in one day to get her bike tuned – and there was something about her. The way she talked about the bike like it was a person, misbehaving. Right then and there, I asked her out, and a long and difficult process thus began.'

I moved to raise my glass but stopped, hid it behind my thigh.

'I have a theory,' he said, rising from the couch, sauntering across the room. 'We men are biologically incompatible with modern society.' He gave me several seconds to absorb this. 'In Roman times, or even a couple hundred years ago, we'd have been more fit for survival. Know why?'

I shook my head.

'Because those societies didn't deny our innate brutality.' He sipped his tea. 'Cockfights, public decapitations, live eviscerations in the coliseum: we thrive on that sort of stuff. Women, on the other hand – all females. Look at cows, monkeys, whales …' He tallied the species on his hand. 'It is biologically advantageous for them to be compassionate. A proven fact. But males must kill, fight off the enemy, inseminate as broadly as possible.'

'Come on, what are you getting at?'

'Monica thinks you might be afraid you're unfeeling.'

'No, it's them that –'

'Shh, you don't need to explain.' He clamped his hand on my knee. 'Would you believe me if I told you I've raped three women?'

I jerked back. 'Jesus, does Monica know?' She was in the kitchen still, with Gillian.

'She does.'

'But she … she was –'

'Yes, yes, I know.' He ran a finger down the spine of his nose. 'Here, let me top you up.' Glug, glug, to the brim. 'Studies show that if you leave a ram with one ewe – the same one – for months, and keep her from getting pregnant so that she still comes into heat, eventually that ram won't so much as sniff her vagina. But put him with a new one, and look out!' *Wham!* Fist to hand.

'What does that have to do with raping women?' I asked, feeling queasy.

'Ladies and gents of the jury, I present to you the prairie vole. This little fella mates for life. Very unusual. He's got something called vasipro– vaso– … Monica! What's the hormone called?'

She popped her head in. 'Vasopressin.'

'Yeah, vasopressin. Makes him faithful. But if scientists block its release, just like the ram, the little devil will screw every new female he can lay his paws on.'

'So we're like voles? Or sheep?'

'A bit of both. Supposedly we're programmed to be relatively faithful, under natural conditions, for just a couple of years. Long enough to raise a baby through infancy. I read this book and it says everything – rape, stalking, homicide – it's all got an evolutionary purpose. But we live in the Age of Compassion, man.'

'The Age of Compassion?'

'Things haven't been this matriarchal since the Stone Age. You don't hunt, unless you're a native or a redneck. Prostitutes are taboo. If someone wrongs you – Jesus, even if someone attacks you – you go to the courts. The courts! Do you see what I'm saying?'

'No.' His image had started to swim with the rest of the room, so I stamped my foot. 'No, I don't. Don't you think it's better that way?'

'Of course. The point is not whether it's better or worse. Only that we guys aren't well-suited to it. Our bottled-up aggression turns into rage. There are consequences,' he declared, with a surprisingly authoritative air, 'to bettering ourselves.'

I nodded disconsolately. 'But I don't feel aggressive.'

'Everyone's different. Let me tell you about me: doctors found my testosterone levels are through the goddamn roof, but my vasopr– vasopressin levels looked on the screen to be pretty low, even after I'd cum. A lot of guys are like that. And listen to this: one doctor I talked to thinks high levels of testosterone actually depress vasopressin production, and vice versa also. What are we supposed to do? Turn off our testosterone?'

Confused, I kept nodding.

'Have you ever wanted to rape?'

My glass slipped from my grasp. 'Oh no – no, here, lemme ... '

'Relax,' he said, with aggravating aplomb. He disappeared into the kitchen and then was back, blotting up my mess, refilling my sticky snifter.

'Hey, lissen, how'd you stop raping then?'

'Like I told you, Mon came along.'

'True love,' I sighed, ready to excuse myself for the night.

'Trev, love doesn't necessarily conquer all. I mean, Mon was my saviour. But she didn't know how hard I was drinking, until one night something happened, I got a bit nuts, you know? Next thing, I was crying and crying – I bared my soul, rapes and all.' He stood and stretched. 'The relief!'

'She forgave you? Just like that?'

'What do you think?' He stamped over to the screen door. 'No, she wouldn't talk to me for a couple of months. I dried up. That's when the guilt set in. Jesus!'

'Did you go find them?'

'Who?'

'The girls, the ones you ... '

'Impossible. They were in Malaysia.'

'Oh.'

'Anyway, meditating twice a day, seeing a shrink. I hadn't touched a drop in a year. But still I felt it in me. In my *nature*.' He thumped his chest. 'My nature needed to change.'

'What are you talking about?' said Monica. She and Gillian joined him on the couch.

'Trev, you're right, society has changed for the better, but men can't adapt that easily. We've got millions of years against us. Of course I should have tried to stop myself with those girls, but it wasn't totally in my control, you see.' He pulled an orange packet from his pocket. 'So I started taking this.'

'What is it?'

'Experimental.' A blister pack of pills. 'My shrink got me on them. They keep your brain rich in that vasopressin that makes you love. The difference is incredible. Once –' he winked at Monica '– once I took two by mistake and we made love – real romantic love – for four hours straight! I bet you don't even know what making love is, Trev.'

'Wassat?'

'Real love, man, for the person you're actually with. Not some hunger nut in your brain, some cluster of vicious thoughts. Love, for every gully and mound of her body.'

Monica smiled dreamily, despite rubbing his leg in a manner more nervous than sympathetic.

I grabbed the arms of the chair and set my sights on Gillian, whose face was blotchy with affection. 'It might be worth trying,' she said, looking at the Bubchucks.

'Hold on a second!' My voice sounded strident and hateful. 'How long do you have to stay on it?'

'Probably forever. I tried to go off when Ben was born, because your natural love chemicals are supposed to kick in then. But it didn't work.'

'Didn't work?'

'At first, yeah. I was going crazy at the hospital, kept on hearing that Neil Young song in my head. You know, *I can love, I can really love, I can really love …*' He essayed a couple of riffs on an air guitar but, finding himself out of tune, faded out.

'Then what happened?'

'After a couple of weeks I had to go back on the pills.'

'You stopped loving your baby after a couple of weeks?'

'No, not Benjy, although he got colic and was driving us both nuts. Monica.'

She tried to cut in.

'Sorry, sorry, that's not what I mean. I didn't stop loving Monica. But after two weeks I stopped *experiencing* my love for her. I started having impulses again. There was this fifteen-year-old who worked in our store and …'

Monica's smile looked strained.

'Well, you know the rest. Ever since, we've been the happiest, horniest couple on the planet.'

'I gotta thhink about it.'

'Trevor, Sandy's on the phone.'

'Huh?'

'It's Mummy.' Monica loomed over me with the morning sun streaming through the window behind her. 'Don't mention any of that stuff we talked about last night, okay?' She handed me the phone.

'Hello.'

'Monkey, are you okay?'

'Hi, Mum.'

'You're in bed still?'

'Just waking up.'

'But you've had a good week?'

'Yes, very nice.' I glanced at Gillian sleeping beside me.

'We're so happy you and Mon are spending time together. Your father and I both think you're really on the mend.' She reminded me I could stop seeing 'that doctor' whenever I wanted, and again cautioned against asking him for advice in that respect, since it was in his interest for me to continue. 'Your father's been talking to his golf friends about some work that might interest you. Once you're back …'

Typical for me when I'm hungover, I felt sick with ill-defined shame. I blurted, 'I love you,' into the receiver, and listened to her wish us a safe journey home.

Meanwhile, 'that doctor' was expecting my call. 'How nice to hear your voice, Trevor. Are you having an enjoyable visit?'

'Dr. Nitz, it's been horrible.'

'Tell me all about it.'

I double-checked to make sure the bathroom door was locked and started ranting in a low voice. 'I feel sick. I'm a prisoner. They treat me like a child.'

Dr. Nitz sighed sympathetically. 'People become quite uneasy around the slightest mental illness.'

'Wait'll I tell you what happened last night!' Dropping my voice further, to a strained whisper, I launched into it, reeling off the hateful details in no particular order, just as they came to mind. Even I was shocked to recall some of them, and Dr. Nitz seemed truly stunned.

'Oh, dear.' There was a moment's silence. 'This Clarence sounds dangerous.'

'And he's married to my sister!'

I could hear some pages flipping. 'This is not a real drug, I don't think. Vasopressin?'

'It's experimental.'

'Experimental?'

I told him about the sheep and the voles.

'No, no, no, we are not sheep, we are not voles – we are human beings, with complex psychologies.'

'But Bob said that if you don't put me on some serious medication they may not believe I'm committed to overcoming my condition.'

'Bob told you! Your condition! Who's the doctor here, Bob, Clarence or Zbigniew? I don't go prescribing willy-nilly for some legal technicality or because your brother-in-law is a rapist. You come into my office next week and we'll review your symptoms, but I don't see any basis …'

'So I'm going to jail then.'

'Jail! Why does Bob say these things? No, come in next week and we'll assess the situation more reasonably. Okay? Are you okay?' For some minutes I remained seated on the toilet, frowning at the phone in my hands.

The rest of that day was, predictably, a nightmare, as the trip played itself out. I couldn't keep down even chicken noodle soup, and I stopped trying to be polite, let alone defend my sanity. Had I dreamt up parts of the night before? The others behaved like nothing had changed. But I felt party to an intimacy as unspeakable as a homicidal swarming, or an orgy, and when anyone got too close, I snarled. Literally, I snarled, alive at last, more desperate than ever to escape. And they responded – yes, they did – even let me stagger alone down to the shore and watch a port-bound trawler, heavy with catch, cleave the glittering sea. Then I turned to find that damned Clarence, with his widest smile yet, squinting in the high noon sun.

Around boulders I scrambled, as fast as my thin soles would allow. He stuck to me, panting, two steps behind, and, sustaining amiability, kept calling for me to stop, stop for a Tylenol, or just a kind word. Over a long bar of rocks, through a confusion of growth, into a cool laneway, where I practically screamed, screamed, 'The glorious shade!' – when what should round the bend but the women, in that bright yellow SUV.

'Where are *you* off to?' Slam, slam.

I collapsed against the hood, with both hands, and heaved. Splashed my shoes. Someone took control of my back.

'Down on your knees.' My elbows struck the ground.

'He's sliding under the truck.'

'That's it, get it out.'

My face was in my own muck.

'Now you feel better, now you're okay,' said Gillian, rubbing my back. Clarence's big white sneakers peered up at me. The baby was crying. The engine was cut.

'Thought you could get away?' said Clarence, as he helped me to my feet.

Sunrise over the mountains is a bit of a disappointment. So small and so bright when it finally breaches the ridge, you throw your hands up and surrender to the full light of day. But when we arrived in Departure Bay, just after 6 a.m., it hadn't happened yet, although the sky was nice and pink. We took breakfast in the terminal.

'Check it out,' smiled Clarence, pointing out a sleek white ship in the strait.

'Our ferry!' I said.

'Nope, an American cruise liner. Our ferry's over there. Docked all night.'

'Oh.' Ours was kind of ugly, its front swung open like a broken jaw and with rust-streaked sides as roughly slapped together as the models I'd misassembled as a boy. I returned to my scrambled eggs, already lukewarm. 'Hey, *you're* drinking coffee, Clarence?'

'It's a special occasion. We don't know when we'll see you again.'

'True.'

He pulled out his orange blister pack.

'Look, look …' cried Monica, pointing to the mainland. Cut against the sky, the mountains resembled an enormous price chart whose precipitous drops ought to have put off the most reckless of investors. At least in jail there'd be no more of that.

Somebody hummed 'Here Comes the Sun,' and sure enough, its leading edge slid into view.

Clarence pushed his pills across the table. 'Wanna try?'

'Nah.'

'Keep them. I'll tell my doctor I lost the pack.'

'How do I know how much I can handle?'

'What, love?' He slapped my forearm. 'Kidding. No, it's standard dose, one pill once a day. My doctor's got colleagues in Toronto. I bet he could get you in on our experiment.'

'I don't know.' I looked at Gillian, who squeezed my knee.

'Could he go back off if he didn't like them?'

'Of course.'

'What about side effects?'

'Nothing. Just more positive emotions.'

'Guys,' said Monica, 'happiness is attainable. Look at us.' They smiled in unison.

'Well …' What *did* I have to lose?

'Come out of your castle, buddy. It's worth the risk.'

I took Gillian's hand, trembling, on my leg, more frightened than me. Okay, I shrugged. Okay? 'It might help my defence.'

She nodded, and continued nodding, absently.

I pressed a pill, no bigger than an aspirin, into my palm.

'Wait,' Monica suddenly put in. 'Don't take it if you don't want to.'

I waved her to be quiet. 'Here goes nothing.'

All three turned away and scrutinized the sun, waiting for me to swallow.

That Man

Rex Weir
Prosecutor
Toronto, Ontario
January 2, 2003

Austin C. Clarke
c/o Penguin Books Canada
10 Alcorn Avenue
Toronto, Ontario M4V 3B2

Dear Mr. Clarke,

First, let me congratulate you on your recent success with *The Polished Hoe*. Having followed your career for fifteen years, since reading the stories in *Nine Men Who Laughed*, I've long anticipated wider recognition for your expanding and rather amusing oeuvre. This has now come to pass. Hardly a week goes by without another of your bold opinions striking my doorstep with a *thunk*; there, your dreadlocked head, a profile, in full colour, spread open on my kitchen table, much food for thought. We have a lot in common, you and I, both of us impassioned defenders of standards, in literature, in life. My convictions, like yours, have more than once occasioned that vague epithet 'snob.' So as one discriminating man to his 'brother,' I appeal to you, beyond the pale of political correctness, in the troubling matter of one Josh M. G. Miller-Corbaine.

You know the name. Of course you do – you invented it. Mr. Josh Miller-Corbaine, a.k.a. … I won't say it. Let us keep up the fiction. It's a credit to your descriptive powers that my contemptible former neighbour proved so immediately recognizable in the above-mentioned collection. Have there been discussions about putting it back into print? Or should we anticipate a 'Collected Works' instead? Your unusual decision to devote not just one, but two, stories – 'A Man' and 'How He

Does It' – to his doings makes me doubt that we've heard the last of him. But before you go launching him on your newly expanded readership, might I suggest that we subject these tales of his to the litmus test of a fresh perspective?

Do you remember writing this: 'Standing erect and sombre as a judge, which he was, was his neighbour who had in all these years never spoken a word to him, not even when the snow covered their adjacent driveways and reduced them to the democratic misery of toiling in the snow with their hands, in wellingtons and with spades?' You, of all people, cannot plead ignorance about the implications of a white 'judge' refusing to speak to his adamantly black neighbour; and transposing our neighbourhood to York Mills, changing our names, mixing up the houses and making me a judge instead of a prosecutor perhaps qualifies as fictionalizing what actually happened, but it doesn't lessen the blow of being slanderously misrepresented. No, in the decade he lived next door to us, Mr. Miller-Corbaine and I socialized on many, many occasions. For a time I would even have called him a friend, if a problematic one.

In lurid detail you relate the semi-secret life he led right under our noses, pleasuring himself with four different white women (their colour is immaterial, but one wonders if his misogyny didn't dovetail nicely with his eternally present culturo-historical grudge – read, racism). His wife, 'Mary,' was a handsome woman whom he practically abused, so appalling was his neglect of her, a fact I became plainly aware of that mild spring morning they first arrived in our neighbourhood, as he strutted out of his golden-hubcapped Cadillac to gloat upon their new house, barking unintelligible commands at her over his shoulder.

The second thing he told me (after his name), when I headed over to introduce myself, was that he was a 'corporation' lawyer. 'How interesting,' I replied. 'I'm a prosecutor myself.' At once he was sweating.

'Well, I practice in Montreal.'

Why then, I wondered, was he in Toronto? I couldn't follow his convoluted explanation, instead noting his nervous tic and his busy hands. Clearly, he wasn't on the level.

In the beginning I quite liked having him around. He spiced up our lives. The first week we invited them for a barbecue, and while my wife, Maureen, insisted on staying inside because of her asthma, probably drawing Mary into a conversation about her other ailments (90 percent of them neurotic), he and I quickly developed the sort of jesting rapport that is punctuated by unspoken *touchés* and can be a barrel of laughs if the score stays more or less even. He poked fun at my apron and my expensive tongs. I told him to stand back from the flames in case his gold-encrusted teeth liquefied. After dinner I gave him one of my prank cigars, which you have to light over and over and over, each time thinking you've got it when you don't – a joke he took a bit too seriously, but recovered from before the evening was through. We parted with congratulatory slaps on the back.

His vulgar ways were really quite astonishing. Stuffing asparagus spikes directly from the platter into one's upturned mouth is one thing, nothing to take offence at; but leaning on one's horn instead of stepping out of one's garish car to press a doorbell is rude and disrespectful. Everything to his taste was 'golden,' a descriptor he applied to the best and the worst Scotch I owned; to fine and, until he got frustrated, prank cigars; to his state of mind any time you asked; and, in practice, to his physical person, so criss-crossed in gleaming watch chains he called to mind one of those heavily ornamented Clydesdales at the Royal Agricultural Winter Fair (to which, incidentally, we invited him and Mary, only to have him spook a team by tossing his program from the box just as it clopped past).

'A Man' purports to establish various quotidian 'facts,' many of which are, simply stated, false. I'll quickly list a few. Ours is a well-to-do neighbourhood. True. It's not far from Forest Hill Village. But the insinuation that we are an island of racists and prigs is wrong. Yes, Mr. Miller-Corbaine was the first black man on our street (alas, we haven't had another), but we had a wealthy Indian family (Miller-Corbaine, with his chip-laden shoulders, wouldn't even speak to Rupinder), a Japanese businessman (rarely home) and two families of Chileans that arrived in the mid-seventies and disappeared less than a decade later. Moreover, we're a stone's throw from Vaughan Road, famous for its Jamaican character, and I'd like to submit, 'as evidence for the defence,' my having regularly – happily – taken lunch, *to stay*, at Albert's Jerk & Patty for years.

In your fiction, our street feels desolate, front yards vacant except for hissing automatic sprinklers and neighbours peeking out through drawn blinds. It's actually one of the safest and most friendly in the city. If one strolls to Ng's Convenience for a quart of milk after dark, children of all ages keep streaming past on bikes and scooters, with peals of innocent laughter, even at that late hour. Disadvantaged children frequently (and lucratively) hold car washes at the local service station. No, Mr. Miller-Corbaine was a problem not because he was black, not even because he was so unapologetically crude; he became such a problem because he was a hateful, bitter man whose rage informed his every move, whether careering down our street in his enormous automobile (he'd swerve within a hair's breadth of our kids) or stumbling about after midnight, defiantly singing his songs.

Both stories, despite their failings ('How He Does It' has even more inaccuracies than 'A Man'), cannot help but shine an unforgiving light on the habits with which he occupied his time when he was supposedly practicing law. We find him motoring around ogling women, or else taking advantage of a rather young schoolteacher, or physically assaulting a sad retiree who each day cooked him lunch and with whom he'd stopped sleeping on her forty-ninth birthday ('I don't like old women,' he told me one hot, confessional night over whisky sours) or carrying on with a rich Jewish woman on the far side of Forest Hill.

He lived off his wife. Her father owned the mining company that her grandfather founded; the latter was instrumental in bringing the symphony and public transit to this city. Mary became a schoolteacher. A gentle, liberal-minded woman who taught Social Studies and Ethnic Cultures, she had eyes that seemed to really listen when you spoke, as we often did, 'discussing the virtues of roses,' as you put it, over the white fence between our backyards, ignoring the butchery her husband had inflicted on her flowers with his high-voltage hedge pruner.

In fact, he may have been lying to you about all the lovers except the Jewish one, whom I deplored from the moment I first laid eyes on her, posing on their front lawn, while he snapped pictures like an amateur pornographer. You state, the third and final time I'm conceded a place in his version of events (all three instances on the same page), that I was raking my 'immaculate' lawn when that happened – it was covered in leaves, the photos would prove this – and that I retreated indoors disapprovingly. I did, certainly I did. For it's one thing to say that you're something you're not. But to publicly humiliate one's wife, especially a perfect angel like Mary, is unforgivable. Your belief that he was nervous and tried to hurry her straight inside doesn't square with my memory: 'Hey, Rexy!' he shouted, winking at me, already revved up to defile that minx, who was hardly more than a teenager. Choked with rage, I *had* to get inside.

She's the one he briefly ran off with, some months earlier, until that poor desperate Mary hunted her down and confronted her in the flesh. We imagine – we pray – our antagonist is doomed, but supposedly he tricks his mistress into believing that Mary is his mentally unstable maid (here 'How He Does It' blithely ends).

Then there was their other encounter, only hours after the photo shoot on the lawn. Quite by accident, whilst hefting a bag of leaves to the curb, I spotted him, through the edge of his living-room window, passed out in an armchair in his three-piece suit. She lay on the floor, naked and easy as Eve in the garden, gazing up at a Monet reproduction. A car door slammed. Voices! *He's sunk.*

That naked slut, splayed on the broadloom. Mary and little Winchester stood frozen in the entrance. She dropped their valises (here ends 'A Man') and fled to our house.

I made it through the back door to the front just in time, pulled her to my heaving chest. Then Maureen appeared and told me to go make supper.

We stayed up most of the night, ignoring his phone calls, his pounding at every window or door within reach. 'You must be strong,' I said to Mary. 'Stay with us until we have him out.' She bawled she couldn't live without him. 'Oh, come on!' I wanted to shake her to her senses. *He hates you!* At dawn she crossed the stiff frosted lawn to where he sat, shivering, on their front steps, and touched his shoulder. They embraced. That he didn't brag to you about this little triumph boggles my mind. Certainly it was a turning point for me.

What exactly are you saying, Mr. Clarke? That he has won? That he has gotten off scot-free to pursue his malignant ways? That *is* the gist of your stories. They conclude without consequence, much like his days. We must see this in its proper light: here we have a man who moves into a community, welcomed but given the simple duty of respecting the members' principles and mores, and not only does he flout common decency, disrupt our peaceful lives and then blackmail me into silence (as we shall see), he goes on to retail stories that make us seem narrow and duped, feeding them to *you*, Mr. Clarke, now a celebrated writer. His colour's not the issue. Why must they always make colour the issue? Part of the reason I love Toronto is for its multi-ethnic character. All that we asked was that he behave respectably, with no explanations owed for the frightfully high crime rate his compatriots brought to this city.

'Come to bed, Rex,' called Maureen. 'It's not your problem.' For the second night in a row – the night after we sheltered Mary – I watched dawn absorb the hard, simple shades of night. Around my desk were scattered balled-up papers, like improperly imagined explosive devices, but in front of me lay a plan, crafty as a shoe bomb. Justice would prevail, poor Winny would learn that one does not behave in the manner of his father; we would revert to happier times. A single piece of damning evidence and we'd settle this matter for good.

The question is, how do you sink a man who is merely the shell of a man? You push him down in a spot that would drown a normal man, but he pops back up, laughs and floats away. Mary could have stripped him of everything, but even when I informed her, based on some enquiries I'd made, that he wasn't a lawyer, she just sat there, regarding her hands, and asked me not to repeat it. She held firm to her conventional notions about his 'feelings of inadequacy,' what she called, without irony, his 'needs,' and to his true colours remained wilfully blind. If she was ever going to wake up to reality, someone needed to give her a dose of tough love. I planned a party to that end.

I sometimes wonder if 'How He Does It' was intended as an ironic commentary on how Mr. Miller-Corbaine sees his behaviour: slightly heroic. Am I right? But, Mr. Clarke, that your folksy narrator, no matter how ingenuous, actually believes his friend to be a teetotaller belongs to the realm of pure fantasy. Mr. Miller-Corbaine was a heavy drinker. I was depending on it for my design to win the day.

First, thanks to a 'mix-up' on my part, the Miller-Corbaines arrived at our party an hour earlier than everyone else. The caterers made his drinks strong. My vexingly anti-social wife had gone to Oakville for the weekend, annoyed that I was throwing another soirée. For decorum's sake, I said her sister was ill, though nothing serious.

"When the cat's away ...' Miller-Corbaine whispered in my ear as we entered the living room.

As soon as we were seated he was waving his arms in the air, haranguing the 'fools' of this city who'd given him another parking ticket. He repeatedly refused to surrender to me even one piece of his multi-layered suit, although beads of sweat, more and more of them, were gathering on his forehead. When finally some other guests arrived, he leapt up and all that salty water broke over his brow. He looked liked he'd been fleeing or weeping. 'Welcome, welcome to Rexy's *cock-tayle*,' he cried, with nuts in his teeth.

Rhonda arrived last.

Rhonda's a very blond call girl – Scandinavian, I believe. A former witness, she once helped me put away a rapist for life. We had since developed something of a paternal relationship, and would go for coffee now and then. I felt like a hero from a Morley Callaghan tale. Of course, for her to feel comfortable, there had to be some give and take, so one afternoon I mentioned my preoccupation with Mr. Miller-Corbaine and his behaviour. I emphasized his neglect of Mary and Winny. With little further prompting, Rhonda hit upon the solution: for a nominal fee she would come to the party I was planning and bait him a bit, if that would help. 'You'd do that for me?' Not a bad idea. 'But don't go too far. I don't want you getting hurt.' I struggled to describe him until she said, 'You mean he's black, right?' Right.

In she strutted on silver shoes, at ten o'clock on the dot. Scintillating, gracious, she'd make the perfect escort. I introduced her to everyone as my legal assistant. When finally I got to Mr. Miller-Corbaine, Mary was sticking close, poker-faced. But soon she relented, such was Rhonda's delicate charm, and with a flurry of smiles and nods tried to make up for her initial coldness. I left everyone to mingle.

You can't control everything, I sometimes tell my (grey-helmeted) assistant. The court of life is the court of law with even fewer controls. And as in any complex experiment, unpredicted factors will affect the outcome. I had formulated the hypothesis that Mr. Miller-Corbaine, cowed by Rhonda's (possibly drug-induced) self-possession and her quasi-professional association with me, would initially restrict himself to sidelong leers, and only as he became quite trashed would migrate to her side of the room to take a stab at her. But I was wrong: he was his usual noisy, jocular self from the get-go and in fact never budged from her thin side. Likewise, Mary hung around, nodding and smiling, knocking back martinis at an unprecedented rate. Not until midnight did she clack through the kitchen, a bit unsteady on her red pumps, and into the bathroom, locking the door behind her. I installed myself nearby and spoke to the chef about the upcoming platter of steak tartare. I felt like the director of a cautionary tale, or a morality play of the most modern sort, with the audience for actors and chance the major player.

When Mary re-emerged, looking flushed, I asked her if she'd join me on the back deck while I smoked a cigar. She equivocated, said she'd be cold, but I gallantly wrapped her in my sports jacket. 'That should keep you warm.' She giggled and wobbled after me.

Only a few pulls into my Montecristo Slim I spotted, through the sliding glass door, Rhonda and Mr. Miller-Corbaine, hip to hip, moving toward what was once a maid's room. I stepped down into the yard. 'Are you frigid?' I asked, and put my arm around Mary's waist. Mr. Miller-Corbaine stopped at the kitchen sink to down several glasses of water. I had to keep her distracted. 'Come down here.'

She put her hands on my shoulders. The cigar she had coquettishly demanded (and had tried to light at the wrong end, without sucking) seemed to have dazed her. She leaned into me, with her breasts in my face. 'What do you think my husband's up to?' she said, her breath hot on my head.

I pleaded ignorance.

'This?' she said, and wiggled her tits. 'Something like this?'

I've always found drunken women embarrassing. 'Why don't you lie down for a few minutes, Mary? There's a bed in the room off the kitchen.'

'How'd you like to lie down in there, Rrrex?'

I humoured her with a few caresses. But my main objective was to get her inside. I did not trust Mr. Miller-Corbaine in that small room with lissome Rhonda, and I didn't want to kill Mary with a scene of mad lust. All I wanted was that she should stumble upon an incriminating situation, suggestive of what was to come, so to speak.

I steered her through the kitchen, past gawking neighbours ('One too many,' I said with a knowing smile). She was like a piece of rubber, firm enough to continue toward the shut door of that cramped room beyond the pantry, but so flaccid you wouldn't say that she moved by her own volition. She was muttering something about 'Joshy' as we approached. Afraid that he'd hear her, I lunged for the doorknob, burst into the room and hit the light switch just as Mary slithered to the floor.

Empty. Not even an indented pillow. I'd moved too fast and botched the whole affair. Mary moaned. Her short red skirt was bunched rather high. I tried unsuccessfully to stand her up. She was too heavy to carry, so I had to drag her by the arms over to the daybed, raise her upper body first and then lift up her legs.

'Rex?' Miller-Corbaine, in the doorway, with bulging eyes and a hand on Rhonda's rear.

'Mary, look!' I shook her foot.

'What, pray tell, are you doing to my wife?'

'She's drunk. I'm taking care of her.'

'Taking care of her, are you? You see that, sweetheart?' he asked Rhonda. 'What he was doing?' She lowered her gaze and grappled his paw off her.

'What exactly are you accusing me of? I'm in here trying to help your wife because you're too busy downing rum and Cokes with my assistant.'

He lurched over and tugged her skirt so that she wasn't so exposed.

'He's not even a lawyer, Rhonda. What are you, Josh? Anything?'

Rhonda blinked at me as though there'd been some kind of misunderstanding, turned on her heels and left.

Mr. Miller-Corbaine firmly shut the door behind her. 'Who told you?'

'I found out myself.'

'Who else knows?'

'Mary.'

'Besides her.'

'Maureen.'

'Anybody else?'

'Not yet.'

He was silent for a moment. 'Okay, here's what we're going to do, Rexy: I will not tell anybody, not even my wife, that you were poking around down there.' He paused, like something new had occurred to him, but then continued. 'And you will not breathe a word of this lawyer business to a soul. Got it?'

'Poking around! How dare you. I can very well imagine that that's what you would have done, with my wife in this position. Raped Maureen. But not me. You can't pin that on me.'

'Your wife? Maureen?' He waved his hand and laughed.

'What's wrong with Maureen?'

'Rexy, if you don't co-operate, I'm telling everyone now.' He started for the door.

'Jesus!' I grabbed his arm. He freed himself. He was halfway out when I caught the back of his jacket.

'Fuck you, Rex.' He knocked me to the ground in the pantry.

'Attention, everyone!' I shouted. People had already clustered in the kitchen, instinctively drawn to where the action was. Now there was dead silence. 'Mr. Miller-Corbaine …' I started saying, propped up on my elbows. He and I stared straight at each other's eyes, like a pair of fatally compromised swordsmen waiting for the other to blink. Son of a bitch. That sort of accusation sticks. 'My friends, Mr. Miller-Corbaine has just informed me that, sadly, he and Mary must move away.' I watched him carefully as I spoke these words, ready to strike if I thought he was going to. His jaw, tensed at first, suddenly relaxed. 'Let's toast them,' I said, and raised my glassless hand. 'We'll miss you.' The guests quietly concurred.

Mr. Miller-Corbaine ignored them. He approached me and offered a hand. I reluctantly took it, because people were still watching. 'Touché,' he whispered, pulling me to my feet. He went into the maid's room, hoisted Mary onto his shoulder and shouted, 'Bye-bye, crackers!' on his way out the sliding glass door.

The very next day he stabbed a 'For Sale' sign in their lawn, herded Mary and Winny into the Cadillac and took off. Some invisible Russians soon replaced them. For a while the house felt like the gap left by a lost tooth before a new one emerges.

Needless to say, the neighbourhood did survive without them. We didn't have any more parties, though, and I upped my caseload significantly, fighting like the dickens for justice, driving that demon and our bitter compromise from my mind to the bang of the gavel.

Then, three years later, I was surveying the discount table in Book City and your paperback caught my eye, Mr. Clarke. You can imagine my outrage upon discovering, on the first page I turned to, my former neighbour, mythologized and spreading lies. It was like finding a tumour after a long and agonizing treatment has been declared successful. I took it home, devoured it, placed my bet on your obscurity and lost.

In truth, those gutless renditions of this tired old saga should reassure me. Their nearly complete exclusion of me and the premature conclusions seem to suggest he understood that maligning me would inevitably bite him in the ass. But did he really come right out and tell you he's not a lawyer? Surely you must have ferreted that out with your writer's instinct. He's probably shaking in his boots now that your name is on everyone's tongue. It's only a matter of time before somebody makes the connection between the fictitious man and the one who swaggers around, lord knows where, still conning his neighbours, diddling a bunch of girlfriends and keeping Mary around just in case. If I were him I'd hop on a plane and disappear for a good long while. But damn it, he's reckless and vain, and probably infamy as a literary hero is more seductive than pretending to be a lawyer until he dies.

Have you considered having *Ten Men Who Laughed*, instead of nine? Or would my words be unwelcome amidst all those bitter screeds? So often intercultural dialogue falters at precisely the place where real ground might have been gained. Let's have a proper airing of grievances, a scrum. You've got my address now – just drop me a line, or even mention my name at a reading, or in the papers, or during one of your very engaging interviews. You'll be surprised at how quickly I come out of the woodwork.

Yours truly,
Rex Weir

ℬ

The Eventual Eponymization
of Tim Pine

'In the following chapters we shall be looking at countless and varied issues from many countries, but none will ever be found again as pure and as noble as the first stamps of all.'
– *Anthony S. B. New,*
The Observer's Book of Postage Stamps

The day Tim Pine was eponymized, everyone but him left the Toronto branch of Providential Insurance Ltd. by five o'clock. For it was a Monday, and winks and innuendo had all afternoon animated their office rapport, anticipating an especially satisfying congress at the Cock & Bull. But Tim, having thoroughly humiliated himself during a lunchhour meeting, hid in his cubicle, re-emerging only when he was quite certain the office was clear. Then he called his wife, Adrienne, and said he was coming home.

They usually hit the Cock & Bull on Mondays to take the edge off the new week with several rounds of beer and baskets of sticky wings, but Tim never attended. They'd spot him rushing past the steamed-up window, heading for home, and Steven Jewel, the joker, might fiddle with his tie and say to Janet Wong, the receptionist: 'Meez Vong, I so sorry I trouble you …,' inciting roars from every chicken-filled maw.

Or 'Have you tried Tim's sausage lately?' A reference to the note Tim periodically posted in the lunchroom: 'Co-workers, I have stored in here very strong sausage and old cheese for snacks. Do sample, but remember to rewrap and return to refrigerator.' There'd be mutterings that the sausage was stinking up the fridge, flavouring the rest of the food. Eventually someone would decide to tell him. But Tim, fearing his meat was about to spoil, each time pre-empted them by polishing off the remaining foot-long coil and a quarter brick of cheese in a single day. This scenario repeated itself every few months, with the same curling note, but nobody had the heart to nip it in the bud. For at bottom, they liked Tim Pine, as one cherishes an outmoded saying, between inverted commas.

Here's how Tim's days begin: 6:54 a.m., he awakens, a minute before his alarm goes off; he whaps Snooze once, to cuddle with Adrienne, until time runs out, three minutes into the hourly news. A peck on her cheek, and he rises to shower, finishing with his feet. When clean, dry, dressed and groomed, with chestnut hair parted rightward, he heads downstairs for breakfast: a small glass of orange juice, a bowl of Raisin Bran, a further half-glass of orange juice and two leisurely cups of coffee with the morning paper. Then it's time to evacuate his bowels.

Conversely, Adrienne Pine (née Alvinczy, second-generation Canadian of 1937 Hungarian immigrants) doesn't have any precise morning routine. Weekdays, she works for the City, transferring land from sellers to buyers, and she does her best to arrive on time. But come Friday night, she always joins Tim in the sweep of their backyard weeping willow, or in their shared study, spreading the day's newspapers around her, setting to work, dirty-blond ponytail bobbing to the tune of her circling and slashing and underlining classified ads that pertain to her fascination with junk. Auction, flea-market, yard-sale junk. Periodically, she might look up, with a knowing smile, and call Tim's attention to some curious phrasing, suggestive of undiscovered treasure, or of garbage disguised. 'You see, Tim?'

'Yes, garbage,' he'll say, or, 'Very nice,' ready to be stood corrected. Then back to his prized collection of stamps: scouring a catalogue, or mounting a new acquisition, or inspecting his pride and joy, a sepia-toned cloth-bound album labelled *Recess-Printed Stamps of the Polish Nation, 1928–1939*.

That fateful Monday Tim kept craning to see past his cubicle partition to the bathroom door at the far end of the hall. He blew noisy exhalations with his rather wide nose, soundlessly stamped a foot, seized the edge of the desk so tightly it trembled.

But the door stayed shut. 'Hurry,' he whispered. He picked up the phone and dialled: 'Miss Wong, I apologize for bother. I must speak with Steven Jool. Please, you will page him for me?'

'Tim, of course.'

'Thank you.'

Janet's voice crackled over the intercom: 'Steven Jewel, Tim Pine needs to speak to you.'

Clop, clop, clop, *marsz, marsz* … the thick, hard soles of Tim's oxfords, on a typical Saturday stroll. He passes High Park metronomically, humming the Polish national anthem: '*Przejdziem Wisłę, przejdziem Wartę* …' Since coming to Canada, loud soles are his basic, if unconscious, requirement from a pair of shoes. Midwinter 1976, he arrived, a young man prematurely stooped from a lonesome, guilt-ridden year in London, with softly sighing boots to take him to dead-end jobs. He'd aver that the first brown oxfords simply caught his eye, that buying them was an extravagant bid for happiness, no inspiration at all. He padded into the store, pointed to the ones in the window, stopped the clerk, repeating, 'No, the pair in the window,' and eagerly tied them on.

Three weeks later he strode on percussive soles into the office of branch manager William Crone and secured himself an accounting position at Providential Insurance Ltd. Then he met Adrienne at a fruit stand, in a landslide of tangerines.

Vignette n. The centre picture of a two-coloured stamp, faded away in tone at its edges so as to allow for variation in register.

'Hello, Bertrand.'

'Tim!' A freckled, paunchy Englishman rose from behind a display case. 'I've been hoping you'd come by.' The two men shook hands.

'Why would that be, my friend?'

'I have a surprise.'

'Oh?'

Bertrand smiled mischievously. 'But let's have a cup of tea first, shall we?'

'Tea? *Nie*, no, I will not enjoy conversation until I see this surprise of yours.'

'Hah! I thought not.' He pulled an envelope from a filing cabinet and set it on the counter.

'Polish?'

Bertrand shook his head. 'Have a look.'

Tim donned glasses and carefully opened it. He gasped. 'The last one.'

'The very last.'

Latvia's last pre-Soviet independent issue, a rich olive photogravure of the national blazon. 'It is so simple,' Tim whispered. 'The light, bring close the magnifier.' It was uncreased, with a very light postmark in the bottom right corner, perforations nicely intact. 'Even better than the one stolen from my suitcase.' He examined it again without the magnifying lamp. 'Yes.'

'I'll put it on your account then. Now you'd like tea?'

'Good, yes.'

They sat in the back, surrounded by tall steel shelves jammed with boxes and books, and over tea discussed purely stampy matters (a highly unusual overprinted Ecuadorian vignette that Bertrand had discovered in a collection he was hired to appraise for an estate; a recent convention he had been to in Chicago; a funny story about an infamous dealer's botched attempt to re-gum rare issues). But Tim was anxious to examine his new acquisition in private, so when his friend moved to refill his cup, he said, 'Just a half,' drained it unceremoniously and excused himself without pretext.

Overprint v. & n. An additional printing (usually wording) applied to a stamp after its original production.

Still Tim watched the bathroom. Nothing. The door stayed shut. What was Jewel doing in there? A picture of Adrienne standing in the garage doorway imperceptibly chattered toward the edge of the desk. This was her fault. Those grapes of hers. He felt sick, his morning routine disrupted.

The phone rang. 'Hello?' he squeaked

'Tim, Steven here. What can I do you for?'

Tim was flabbergasted. 'Oh! Jool … yes, Steven … ha, ha, ha, Mr. *Jool*. But who is in the … ? A mix-up – I must speak with Mr. Jeral.'

'Who?'

'No, no, it's … I make mistake. You I think need, but …'

'Who's Mr. Gerald?'

'Perhaps, or no, no … is okay.'

'Mr. Gerald, you say?'

'I don't remember, Steven, but I must go.' At a loss as to the source of the confusion, he raced down the hall and entered without even a preparatory inhalation.

Just as Tim, homebound with his treasure, climbed onto a westbound streetcar, a thick-fingered, pot-bellied Portuguese man was helping Adrienne load a jug of young red wine and a cast-iron cogwheel into the trunk of a rented car. 'See you at seven then, Carlos,' she called out the window. Fingers crossed that Tim would be out, she motored across Dundas and parked the sky-blue compact in their driveway.

Shortly, he came hurrying down their street, the stamp held firmly, gently, beneath his left arm, a perfectly round orange pumpkin pressed to stomach with his right. His gaze was fixed on the rear of a car, visible through their defoliating hedge. He examined it with a '*Co?*' before continuing inside.

'Adrienne.' He smelled paprika. 'Adrienne!'

'Hello,' she called.

He hurried to the kitchen, at the back of the house. 'Vot? …' He was still out of breath. 'What is the meaning?'

'Oof ut?' She had been chopping onions, and turned big wet eyes on him, with a chunk of bread jammed between her teeth, supposed to keep her from tearing up.

'Of that car?'

'Mmh mim,' she said.

'*Co?*'

She signalled for him to wait, and then finished with the onions while he expatiated on his surprise at finding a car in their driveway. The chopping stopped. She chewed and swallowed. 'You have to wait until six. I have some very exciting news.'

Se-tenant adj. Joined together. The term is applied to stamps of different design printed together, often for booklets.

'Ready?' Adrienne stood in the study doorway with her arms akimbo.

He shrugged, and crossed into the kitchen to pour a glass of vodka. 'I'm not sure.'

'Well, I'm going to have some Concord grape wine I've got out in the garage.'

'Oh?' They went out and Tim eyed the jug suspiciously. '*Skąd*? It is from where?'

'Just bring it in. I'll tell you.'

Inside he tilted it to her glass and sniffed. 'Grapey.'

'Wow! That is *good*. Try.'

'Mmm, yes, very nice.' He had some more. 'Effervescent.' He sat at the table. 'What about the car?'

'You like the wine?'

'Yes, I sayed so. Very nice.' He drank his vodka nervously, crossed his leg and bobbed a slippered foot. 'The car?'

'Well, I bought the wine, along with a terrific cogwheel, from a marvellous Portuguese fellow named Carlos.' She took a swig. 'We talked for over an hour, and I tried his wine – I just thought it was wonderful. Then Carlos tells me about this little farm his brother has on the south side of the lake, east of Hamilton – just lovely. And before you know it I rented a car and we're all going down to press grapes tomorrow morning.'

'*Vot?*' Tim knit his brow.

'We're going to make wine with Carlos and his brother.'

'*Po co?* Why we want to do that?'

'Oh, come on, Tim. The harvest is coming in.' She plucked a piece of fruit from the air.

'So?' He shut his eyes and visualized the next day as planned: remounting some stamps, detailing the Latvian find in his philatelic diary; a walk in the park in the afternoon, with Adrienne if she was in the mood; the pumpkin needed to be carved.

She sighed. 'Am I going on my own then?'

'*Nie*, on your own? Why you say that? *Nie* on your own.'

'So you're coming?'

'Okay, okay, *zgoda*.'

Adrienne clapped and wandered toward the door to the garage before she said, 'We'll pick up Carlos at seven then.'

'Seven! In the morning?'

'Of course.'

'No, why so early? Not seven. Call Carlos and say eight. I cannot go at seven. Why seven?'

She explained that they had to be there early if they were going to help pick, that it was hardly an hour away, that she hadn't Carlos's number, that she didn't know Carlos's brother; and wasn't the wine the very best he'd ever had, wouldn't it be exciting to make their own, bottles and bottles of the stuff? 'We have got to get away, Tim. Please, just tomorrow.'

'Okay, okay.'

At Providential Insurance the men's bathroom has three stalls. Tim beetled into the first but found the toilet brimming murkily. The middle door was jammed. And the third door opened on a bowl smeared with brown swirls, a wet constellation sprayed across the seat. He stalled. Toilet paper – one-ply – would be too flimsy to properly mop up the urine. Incredibly, he redoubled his sphincteral command, and fed a quivering hand into the paper-towel dispenser by the sinks, succeeding only in ripping off dime-sized scraps between grasping thumb and forefinger. '*Nie, Nie, Nie* …' he whispered in high register, and grappled with its face. He fingered the catch. There had to be a trick to this. He dug into his inside jacket pocket, produced a shiny silver pen and pried.

Carlos's brother Jose's farm lay on rising land at the base of the Niagara Escarpment, with vines rambling down an easy slope. 'Is important that you do not pull the bunches and strip the bark,' he said. 'We use clippers.' He handed them out. 'Only good, dark grapes.' He snipped a fat bunch to demonstrate.

Tim pointed to one that was dark at the base but faded into dusty greenness toward the tip.

'Nope.'

Initially, he lacked confidence, shivering in the chilly breeze, and his hand wouldn't relax into the snipper's grip. But he was pleased he'd worn his high-top, zip-up galoshes, in spite of Adrienne's earlier snickers and Carlos's sidelong glances. The sun continued climbing, according to the order of things, and things warmed up, including Tim's fingers, which before long moved about the vines with surprising dexterity. Expertly, he'd cradle a bunch in his purpling left hand, snip with a satisfying snap, and hardly had the blades grazed open before he'd be on to the next, eating any fruit that fell in his path.

The dispenser's face dropped open. Tim grabbed the stack of paper and hurried into the stall, which locked with a clack.

There was no hook. Exasperated, he hung his jacket over the door. He flushed the toilet, without any effect on the brown vortex, wiped down the seat, padded it with paper and dropped his pants and person in a single motion that ended in a medley of private noise, including a groan.

Cocooned in his own fragrance, he relaxed. He forgot his fear of strange dung, ignored the fouled device he was perched upon; and his mind dallied with intimate matters: a litho-graphed 1964 Polish stamp of a black cat he had a lead on; his father's ongoing, if increasingly senile, exhortations that he return to Krakow. He tallied how much they'd saved for a visit, chuckled to himself about Adrienne and her cogwheel, felt badly for giving her such a hard time about yesterday's trip.

'Time for lunch!' called Jose, descending from the house with a magnum of wine and a basket of bread and cheese. Adrienne clapped with delight. Tim quickly settled down on the grass and reached for food.

Suddenly all eyes turned to him, as to the sound of distant thunder. He blushed and heard his stomach rumble again. 'Hungry.' With a weak cough, he took more bread, to stuff himself according to some logic of reabsorption. Cups of wine were passed around, which he wisely declined. His blue orbs darted from his watch to the stacks of emptied bushels awaiting attention, to the harsh eye of the apical sun; but he was firm in his resolve to override his silly body's demands and avoid the revolting ceremony of a gluteus maximal christening at the waters of a stranger's bowl.

The bathroom door swished open, briefly admitting the whirring and clicking of the photocopier next door, and sighed shut. *Clop, clop, clop, zzzip,* someone went to work at the urinal, with a tentative splash, a sniff – *blaaat,* breaking wind – sigh, and at last, *squirrrrrr* … Tim couldn't help listening to each successive stage, even anticipating the final droplets: *plink … plink, plink. Now flush,* he thought, *flush.* No flush happened. Just an overconfident zip and the anonymous barbarian clomped away with unwashed hands to spread sickness throughout the workplace.

Bliss had decidedly ended. He stood and cleaned himself thoroughly. With a last piece of paper he knocked his ring of protection from the seat into the bowl before flushing.

Watermark n. The semi-transparent pattern that becomes visible when paper is held against the light, or put face downwards on a black surface. It is sometimes merely an indication of the maker's name, but more often a security device.

So back to work it was, without relief. For two hours Tim gasped, strained and pinched, picking grapes more slowly but with what seemed to be studied deliberation and a most cautious step. By three o'clock they'd stripped the vines of ripe grapes. The tractor chugged with its load into the shed, where the crusher waited, and it was time to de-stem.

Tim walked very slowly up the dirt path, his face marbled beneath a fringe of fallen bangs.

'What's the matter?' said Adrienne. 'You look wretched.'

'I must go,' he whispered.

'Aren't you enjoying yourself?'

He grabbed her hand. 'No, it's that I must go.' He signalled downward with his eyes and twisted his hips.

Adrienne understood. 'Can you make it home?'

He nodded.

'Are you sure?'

'Yes, I can make it, but we must leave right now.'

She led him to the shed and explained to Carlos and Jose that he felt sick. They had to go. Tim shrugged apologetically. Carlos pleaded with them. He showed Adrienne the crusher, turned the handle and extolled the sugar content of the grapes. Then he touched Tim's forehead and urged him to go inside. But the couple were unbudgeable. When Tim, impossibly, paled a further shade, the brothers agreed, they'd better go, if that's what they thought best. Carlos would stay and take the bus tomorrow. After an exasperating number of warm words and promises, the Pines performed a five-point turn and their rented compact scudded, like a misplaced scrap of sky, down the rough gravel drive, as Tim lurchingly sought to balance the urgency of his requirement against the potentially calamitous impact of potholes and rills.

Whether the toilet had been partially plugged before Tim got to it is a question he would later put to Adrienne. The aforementioned swirls suggested heavy use, but the water had been clear, and he'd noticed nothing unusual with his advance flush. This time the contents gurgled and started to rise. Backed up against the door, he fumbled the lock open, eye on the bowl, and twisted out of the stall with his belt still undone, as the soiled, matted surface paused at the rim before overflowing, just a trickle. He let the door slam shut. He listened. The water had stilled. He washed his hands and fastened his belt.

What was he to do? It didn't seem right to flee. The paper-towel dispenser was, of course, empty now, the remaining stack absorbing whatever fluids made it to the floor. He was drying his hands on his pants when Steven Jewel appeared.

'How you doing, pal? Did you get that sorted out?'

Tim's hands flew up. 'Ah, oh, Steven, fine. Yes, everything.' Bright red cheeks, nervous *heh-heh-heh*.

Tête-bêche adj. & n. (of a postage stamp) Inverted in relation to one another.

He was rustling down the hall, straight for his cubicle, when the office air struck him as cool and peculiarly fluid.

His jacket.

'*Nie!*' He'd forgotten it over the door. '*Cholerny świat!*' he cursed, and stared at the bathroom.

'What's that, Tim?' a soft voice inquired. 'Did you find Steven?'

'Ah, oh yes, Mees Vong. Hello. Of course, yes, fine.'

'Is everything all right?'

'Oh, yes, it is fine. I just remember something I forget.'

Janet Wong tracked his unhappy looks to the bathroom door, which Steven Jewel presently opened, with Tim's jacket slung over his arm.

'Tim, you forgot this in the shitter,' he called, striding toward them. He winked at Janet and held out the jacket. 'Anyone would recognize it.'

It was true, Tim always wore one of two brown tweed jackets, tightish, with elbow patches. He stared at the limp piece of him, just the wrong colour for the occasion, and rattled off some phonetic improvisation, until, pausing, he signalled with both hands that Steven should hold the jacket for just a moment longer, and then launched back in with words: 'You see, I find myself very forgetful today. I put my jacket there when I find other stall jammed. Of course, I pulled because two were plogged ...' A conspiratorial glance, an arc, between Steven and Janet accelerated his explanation: 'Okay, Steven, then I decide nofing vorth my vorry, vosht my hands ...' He raised them, palms out, and they weighed into the explanation with grasping motions. 'But natchurally ...'

Steven Jewel rubbed his contorting mouth. 'Good, good,' he said, and took a step away.

Tim grabbed his arm. 'It vas like that, the toilet, plogged, already!'

Janet stared at the floor.

'It vas like that!'

'I have to go!' Steven blurted, pushing Tim's jacket into his helpless hands and barging past. With stifled gasps, he hurried to his office at the end of the hall and shut the door before exploding with laughter.

'Tim.' Janet touched his elbow, pointed to his shoe: a streamer of toilet paper, six squares long, half-encircled him.

Adrienne Pine was busy transferring land when a co-worker reported, 'Tim's on the line.'

'Tell him I'll call right back.'

'It sounds like something's wrong.'

'Oh?' She picked up the phone.

'Adrienne! Your cogwheels and treeps to country. What ideas you have! Now we have meeting, and I say what? Ruined, all is ruined. Jool and Miss Wong, Crone ... '

'Calm down, Tim. Stop. What's happened?'

'We have meeting about bathroom, which I must explain.'

'Well, please explain then, Tim – I can't understand what you're talking about.' Tim launched into his messy predicament. He glossed over some details, but the gist of the matter was communicated well enough, and Adrienne couldn't help giggling at least once.

'You think this funny also? This is not funny. Now we have meeting and I say what?'

It turned out that Bill Crone had announced an informal lunch meeting, which Tim was certain pertained to the overflowing toilet. What was he to say? She tried to convince him the meeting had nothing to do with that. He repeated, 'It is, it is.'

'Well, you have nothing to be embarrassed about. Everyone plugs a toilet now and then.'

'Not like this. And the jacket! Jool has a very big mouth.'

'No, I don't believe this meeting can be about a plugged toilet. No way.' She told him he'd best act like nothing happened.

Tim's apologia trickled from his fingers with deceptive facility. He tinkered with a word or two, added and removed a comma, but ignored the intermittent grammar-check underline, reassured, as always, by a quadrilingual poet acquaintance's hot response, some years earlier at a Polish-Canadian Christmas party, to Tim's enthusiasm for this function: 'Pay attention to that and you write like a robot.' Tim certainly didn't want that, so thereafter he tended to admire his solecistic turns of phrase rather than 'correcting' them. Now he printed the document and, with glasses riding low on his nose, confirmed that it was good. He shucked his backup jacket of its dry-cleaner wrap and felt ready.

> **Bogus** n. A stamp pretended to have been issued but which never was. Sometimes the country-name is either fictional or that of an uninhabited island.

The boardroom was empty. Sitting near the door, Tim ate his lunch exceedingly slowly, determined to draw it out as long as would be necessary. Between nibbles he practiced his speech in whispers.

'Tim, how's tricks?' Steven patted him on the shoulder and took a seat at the far end of the table. Tim nodded, indicating with vigorous mastications and hand signals that his mouth was full. Others trickled in. When Bill Crone arrived, the meeting commenced.

'There are a few things I want to briefly discuss,' he said, delicately fingering his thinning brown curls. 'First of all, the upcoming blanket increase in auto premiums ...' He passed around some information. 'Secondly, the Christmas party. We need a planning committee.'

Janet volunteered first, several others followed suit, but not Tim.

'Thirdly, the state of the washrooms.'

Just as he had guessed. In fact, he was relieved. He glanced at Steven Jewel and raised his hand. 'Mr. Crone, I must say something before you.'

'All right, Tim, go ahead.'

He stood up and adjusted his glassed. 'My friends, I am a clean and careful man. In my years with Providential Insurance, I used toilets several times only. Every time I flushed and have never leaven a single mess. I encountered today two toilets full to brims. But on one door I hanged my jacket, because the middle one was jammed, which I gave a hard pull, to no success, so I use urinal instead. Then I forget my jacket, which Mr. Jool kindly retrieves, which now must go directly to cleaner's. The situation is not sanitary and we must change.' He read it word for word, eyes glued to the page, while puzzled looks shot back and forth across the table. Then he sat and, seemingly oblivious to the room full of people, fetched a sigh, pinching the bridge of his nose.

A deep vertical furrow bisected Bill Crone's brow. Somebody coughed. Finally, Crone, failing to suppress a smile, said, 'Thank you, Tim, for your responsibility in the washroom. I'm sure we all appreciate that, the cleaning staff especially. And I share your concern about a general lack of care. This morning poor Maria was furious about having to deal with the mess in there.' He shook his head. 'Come on, guys, let's try to be more responsible, why don't we?' Everyone agreed and the meeting ended.

Tim didn't leave his cubicle the rest of the afternoon. He fiddled with his bent pen, recalculated some numbers that had been causing him problems and, only when he was certain the office was clear, called Adrienne to say he was coming home.

At the Cock & Bull, Steven Jewel and Roger Sacks, silent occupant of the 'jammed' middle stall, had everyone in stitches as they pieced together Tim's misadventure, concluding with a heavily accented reading of the speech that he'd forgotten in the boardroom.

'Hey,' said Janet Wong, 'why did Tim get me to page you this morning?'

Steven shrugged. 'He said it was a mistake and hung up. He sounded in a rush.'

'Same when he talked to me!' A twinkle in her eye. 'Like he was pining to go.'

Eureka.

In spite of a general disdain for puns, this one captured the insurance workers' imaginations: they repeated it again and again, pursuing Tim from his cubicle to the boardroom, right into the bathroom, where, in one of those bursts of creativity that are the high-water mark in any civilization's development, they hammered out his bracingly incongruous eponym, a neologism still in common currency at Providential Insurance today:

Pine v. to plug a shitter.

Not to be confused with:

Pine[1] n. any evergreen tree of the genus Pinus (family Pinaceae), native to northern temperate regions, widely used for furniture, pulp, turpentine and tar.

Pine[2] v. (usu. foll. by for, after, or to + infin.) to long eagerly; to yearn.

Acknowledgements

Heartfelt thanks to Shannon Bramer, Maria Scala and my parents, for their support. Thanks also to the Eastend Arts Council (Saskatchewan), the Banff Centre for the Arts and Wired Writing Studio, Annabel Lyon, and to Alana Wilcox and Coach House Books.

'Just Watch: An Apologia': An earlier version of this story appeared in *PRISM International*.

'Semicolon, Coma, Period: A Treatise on Punctuation': Thank you to the late Jane Clark, former librarian at Robarts and family friend, for helping me flesh out Teddy's working life. Sinclair misquotes from a Rimbaud letter that is translated in the introduction to the edition of *Illuminations* referenced within the story.

'Greg Denton Dons Golden Threads in Anticipation': An earlier version of this story appeared in the *Nashwaak Review*. In 2001, Canadian artist Greg Denton made an effort to contact sixty-three people in North America who shared his name, hoping to create a series of paintings of Greg Denton by Greg Denton without doing a self-portrait. The project is as yet incomplete and has not been exhibited. Though inspired by the initiation of Greg Denton's project, and although the title character and characters within share his name, this story is a work of fiction. It quotes from the invitation to Greg Denton's 2000 project, titled *anyone lived …, 400 Consecutive Portraits Painted from Life*.

'Distance': Dr. Nitz quotes and misquotes from *Introduction to Type* (5th ed.) by Isabel Briggs Myers (Palo Alto, CA: Consulting Psychologists Press, 1993). Trevor refers to *Madness: A Brief History* by Ray Porter (New York: Oxford University Press, 2002). The epilogue is an excerpt from a BMO Nesbitt Burns 2002 quarterly investment report.

'That Man': Thanks to Austin Clarke for his editorial contribution, good humour and co-operation.

'The Eventual Eponymization of Tim Pine': Tim Pine was inspired by Vladimir Nabokov's endearing Timofey Pnin, protagonist of the novel *Pnin*. The philatelic definitions are taken from *The Observer's Book of Postage Stamps*, by Anthony S. B. New (London: Frederick Warne & Co. Ltd., 1967). The definitions of *pine* are from the *Canadian Oxford Dictionary* (1998).

About the Author

David Derry lives in Toronto with his wife and two daughters, and works as a contract analyst.

Typeset in Arno Pro
Printed and bound at the Coach House on bpNichol Lane, 2009

Edited and designed by Alana Wilcox
Cover paintings excerpted from *Out of Date: 365 Self Portraits*
   (1999, oil on panels, 6" x 8" each) by Greg Denton,
   courtesy of the artist
Author photo by Shannon Bramer

Coach House Books
80 bpNichol Lane
Toronto ON M5S 3J4

416 979 2217
800 367 6360

mail@chbooks.com
www.chbooks.com